# TANGLED UP IN LOVE

## TRINITY LAKES ROMANCE BOOK NINE

CAROLYN MILLER

CHAPTER ONE

M*arch 26, 2024*

"Oh, thank you, my dear. You've been an angel."

"No problem." Ellie Reilly smiled at the elderly woman as she passed over the small floral bag she'd just retrieved from the plane's overhead compartment.

"I have enjoyed having someone looking after me, and then for you to wait while everyone else disembarks? You have a good heart. Thank you, dear." Florence—her seat companion these past five hours—patted Ellie's arm. "I'm sure you'll be getting home soon."

Home? Ellie's smile stiffened as the waiting flight attendant assisted Florence to the exit and the waiting wheelchair.

Why did the thought of returning home bring an equal amount of joy and fear? Ellie Reilly—Eloise Anne Reilly on her passport—hitched up her backpack and surveyed the line of passengers waiting to deplane. Here at the Tri-Cities airport she was now three flights from London, which was approximately three flights too far away from where she wanted to be. Three flights she'd spent the past five thousand plus miles worrying this exact question. Because, yeah, there was joy in the anticipation of seeing family and friends, and sleeping in her own bed, using her own bathroom, even if the peach décor of the ranch bathroom was dated. But this mingled with the fear that now she'd finally seen something of the world, she'd be expected to immediately settle back into the small-town life of Trinity Lakes and be content. The Reilly ranch. The familiar. The ordinary. Like one sip of the wider world was all she was destined to drink.

But now she'd had a taste she wanted it all. These past eleven weeks had only increased her thirst. And while Europe in winter meant an unfortunate number of museums were closed, she'd still had the chance to see so many more wonders than she'd ever dreamed possible.

Truth be told, she'd never dared to dream that a trip to Europe could happen, until her brothers had banded together and given her a much-belated twenty-first birthday gift of a vacation abroad. "Go see Europe and England," Mitchell, her second oldest brother, had said, when he'd handed her the check at Christmas.

She'd been stunned, unable to believe what she was seeing. Somehow her brothers had recognized her secret dream and made it come true. "But I thought we were still struggling."

"The ranch is doing better now," Jackson, her third eldest brother, had said. "Since Liam Darcy started renting the lower acres for the solar panels we're doing okay. So, this is partly a thank you from all of us for all your hard work over the years, and partly a belated twenty-first birthday gift."

Belated by four years but she didn't care. Her usually non-demonstrative brothers had been inundated with hugs and happy tears, even though Dermott, brother number one, had received his portion of hugs and tears virtually, over Zoom.

He'd once again celebrated Christmas with his wife and two kids all the way over in the Independence Islands, off the coast of South Carolina.

Jackson had even given her a separate check for one thousand dollars, insisting she reserve it for clothes. "I know it's not nearly what you're entitled to, but something is better than nothing, right?"

"But I don't need new clothes," she'd insisted. Jackson might say the Reilly ranch was doing okay, but it seemed hard to believe there'd been such a dramatic turnaround in half a year.

"Then spend it on shoes." Lexi Franklin, Jackson's girlfriend —but as of February 14 his fiancée—had given Ellie a wink.

"She's right," Cooper, her youngest brother—two years older —had drawled. "If that door opens, then run through it, sis. Don't knock back a gift-horse and all that."

So she'd spent it, and okay, used *some* of it on souvenirs for her brothers, mom and friends. Like Lexi. And next-door neighbor Georgia. And Jasper.

Jasper. Her heart twinged. He'd been the only one who hadn't cheered on her good fortune with undiluted joy. Sure, he said he was excited but she'd also sensed a bit of hesitation, and his hug goodbye on New Year's Eve had been a little strained. Too quick, not nearly long enough for her to soak up her best friend's warmth, Jasper's smile had appeared forced, his blue eyes drained of animation. It had proved the one off-key note in an otherwise perfect send off. Even her mom had come to the airport to wave goodbye.

She smiled. Her mom's health had improved so much of late, mostly thanks to Lexi's careful nursing. Lexi's new job at the tiny Trinity Lakes hospital meant Ellie had been concerned about what her absence from the ranch would mean. But weekly video calls with Mom, Jackson and Lexi had reassured, and their requests to keep having fun had meant she had. Even as she'd questioned why Jasper had only answered twice. She hoped he was okay...

The line finally started moving, and she smiled at a little girl holding her dad's hand.

"You look like a turtle," the girl said, tilting her head, pointing to Ellie's backpack.

"I feel like one." Ellie hoisted her backpack higher. "It's pretty full." Stuffed full of trinkets, clothes and memories. But she didn't feel turtle-like only because of the bulkiness. After the fast-paced life of the past two-and-a-bit months, already she was feeling the slow drag of a different weight the closer she neared home. Jackson would meet her, and while she'd be super glad to meet him, she knew seeing him would lead to the inevitable weight of obligations to the family, the ranch, even Mom. And even just articulating that felt so disloyal, especially after their generosity in sending her on this trip of a lifetime.

Nobody ever mentioned that. How the "trip of a lifetime" suggested it was only one such trip. And now her appetite had been whetted for more. So just how was a girl with a taste for history—who had walked through ancient monuments from the Parthenon to Stonehenge—ever supposed to settle down in Trinity Lakes, whose non-indigenous history barely stretched back two hundred years? And even though she loved Trinity Lakes, now she'd seen some of the great cities of the world— London, Paris, Rome—her small town felt exactly that. Small.

She sighed, rolled her eyes at herself—poor her, not—and managed another smile for the little girl. It was okay. God would direct her paths. She'd been listening to the podcast by that Aussie worship singer, Sarah Maguire—Sarah Walton—and she'd heard this very topic discussed the other day. So she knew that she could trust God with her future. Her heart and mind might know it, even though her soul seemed to be taking a while to come on board.

Their slow procession took them past a coffee shop, and her

lips twitched. Okay, she *was* looking forward to a coffee at Trinity Lakes' Bellbird Café. Now she'd traveled to Europe she understood the difference between a real coffee, like what was served at the Bellbird by the Aussie owners with Italian heritage, and what her tastebuds now recognized as the bitter brew served in much of the US. She passed a sign banning the transport of guns in hand luggage—something which always drew a horrified gasp from the Aussies she knew, like Lexi, who wondered how it could even be a question—and tugged her jacket closer.

It was cold, the large windows showing dirty snow tracked around the runways. The calendar might say spring, but if there was this much snow here, it probably meant the ranch would be two feet deep in white. Awesome.

She trudged through the gates to the exit and baggage claim, peering around for Jackson. His height and curly brown head should be easy to spot. But he wasn't here. She dug out her phone, switched it off airplane mode, and winced as a dozen messages came flying in. Wunderbar.

"Ellie?"

She glanced up, her heart leaping. "Jasper!"

Then, as if all doubts and weight had fallen away, she raced over to give her best friend a hug.

He opened his arms and smiled, and she dumped her backpack and threw her arms around him, her head buried in his neck as she savored his warmth and comfort. So things were okay with him. Thank goodness. It was hard enough coming back without feeling like she'd lost one of the most important pieces of her life in Trinity Lakes.

"I missed you," she whispered against his neck.

His arms tightened. "I missed you too."

Her heart fluttered at the rasp of his voice, a deep huskiness she'd never heard before. She was about to pull away, when his hands slid up her back, up to the tangled knotted dark mess that was her hair. She probably smelled bad—all those flights meant it felt like years since she'd last showered—but he didn't seem to care, so she relaxed and closed her eyes. Then grew aware of the way Jasper clutched her, flush against himself, his strong chest against hers, his scent clean and cool, the bristles of his chin against her cheek, the caress of his hand along her back and hair. Her heart thudded. If she didn't know better, she'd almost think—

"I'm so glad you're home," he murmured.

"I kinda got that impression," she teased. "If you hug me any longer people will think we're an item."

"Oh." He released her abruptly and pulled back. Emotion was in his eyes, then he blinked, and rubbed a hand over his face, his gaze sliding away from hers. Down to her dumped backpack, lying forlornly, like the shell of a poor upside-down turtle, on the tiled floor. "This all you got?"

Her heart twisted. What had just happened? Whatever that... moment... had been she'd just killed it with an ill-timed jibe. And now she really wanted to know just why he'd hugged her so long. Like, *really* wanted to know. But asking such a question felt dangerous, and anyway, her mouth had filled with rocks, forcing her to clear her throat. "Uh, no."

He nodded, not looking at her as he picked her backpack up with one hand. She'd always thought herself strong, but even her hard-won muscles couldn't compete with Jasper's strength from doing building contracting work, and working alongside his dad at Cohen's Hardware these many years.

But while he might carry her backpack she felt weighted anew with the unspoken, with the dread of expectations, and a strange certainty she'd just killed something that had barely taken its first breath. And so, chest tight, she followed him to the baggage claim.

———

TALK about a claim on his heart. Jasper carefully exhaled, all too conscious of the woman walking beside him. How to explain that moment before? He couldn't. Except that in that moment of seeing her after nearly twelve weeks apart—yes, he'd counted the days—he had come to realize she was branded on his heart. Ellie Reilly was his person. She'd always been, ever since his family had moved here when he was in elementary school. There might be traces of snow outside, but he'd always considered effervescent Ellie like the sparkle in the summer sun that just made each day brighter and more shiny, while he was more easygoing, temperate, like a mild spring day. Time apart had only deepened his affection into something he thought ran awfully close to love.

But he could never admit that. The way she'd looked at him questioningly before scared him. And he couldn't risk this friendship breaking. So he needed to play it safe. Play things cool. Play things the way they'd always been.

Ellie was his best friend. And they were *only* friends, as she'd just made clear. That was all she wanted, so that was all they'd be. Even if he'd long dreamed for more. So he'd just have to pretend he was fine with being friends, because he really was. Well, he would be.

They reached the baggage claim where one of the two conveyors slowly bumped and groaned its way around. Pasco's airport was small, only five gates, so the waiting passengers were all from Ellie's flight.

"Which bag is yours?" he asked, gravel in his tone. He cleared his throat. Man, what was wrong with him?

"Um, that one." She pointed to a nondescript black bag with gold ribbons around the handle. "But it's okay. I'll get it."

"It's fine." He placed her backpack down then shouldered his way past the clutch of phone-gazing travelers and plucked Ellie's bag from the conveyor belt.

"Oh, young man, would you mind?" An elderly lady in a

wheelchair, clutching a floral bag, pointed to a purple monster of a suitcase.

"Sure." He hoisted it off and set it upright so her companion could wheel it easily, then picked up Ellie's bag.

"Thank you." She beamed an old lady grin at him, then smiled at Ellie who'd drawn near, and was wearing her backpack again. "Your boyfriend is so strong."

Jasper coughed, as Ellie's cheeks flamed to the pink he was sure decorated his own.

"He is, isn't he?" Ellie eyed him, mouthing a "sorry" at him, before turning back to the woman with a spontaneous hug and a "Bye, Florence."

He shrugged, glancing away, pretending to be focused on the exit while he pretended Ellie's silent apology didn't cut deep. Of course him being her boyfriend wasn't true, so it shouldn't hurt. But sometimes truth stung all the same.

Jasper waited until Ellie had completed her farewells—as per usual she seemed to have made friends with half the crowd here —and then guided her to the exit.

"You should brace yourself," he said as they neared the second lot of glass sliding doors. "The recent low means it's still pretty icy outside."

"Okay—ooh!" Ellie did a full body shiver as they exited, tugging out his smile. "How far away did you park?" Her breath wisped white in the cold.

"Just there." He beeped unlocked his Chevrolet truck, hurrying beside her to make sure she didn't slip. Sure she'd lived in these parts longer than him, but he'd be darned if she was going to lose her footing on the icy sidewalk on his watch. Especially when he'd basically twisted Jackson's arm to come. Fat lot of good that had done. He should've stayed home.

He shook his head at himself—what kind of pathetic whiner was he?—and placed her bag in the truck's bed, then hefted her backpack in too. "Get in."

"The bed or the cab?" she teased, before grinning and scooting to the passenger door, leaving him to check her bags were secure.

He braced his hands on the cold metal sides. He could do this. Pretend his heart wasn't a mess of conflicting emotions, pretend his confusion wasn't real, or that he wasn't still embarrassed by that too-long hug from before. What had he been thinking? That they actually were a couple separated for too long? Maybe that's what the old lady had seen, and made an assumption like the one he'd dreamed would one day be real.

"You coming?" Ellie's voice was faint.

"Yeah," he called. "God, help me," he muttered as he slowly moved to the driver's door. He needed divine help to drive the next hour or so without making any more mistakes. Was that possible with Ellie seated a foot away? He hoped she hadn't misread too much into that hug, that she just thought he'd wanted to get warm or something. *Please, God.* He'd die before admitting the truth. That he'd missed her something fierce, that he'd gotten so desperate he'd even recently looked up weekend flights to London to see her. But that pipedream had plummeted to reality given he now had neither money nor time, especially given his dad's recent health battles. Not that he'd told Ellie about that. He wondered if anyone else had.

The cab filled with uncomfortable silence as he merged onto US-12 East towards Walla Walla. But maybe he didn't have to talk. After all those flights she had to be tired, right? He peeked across. She grinned at him, oblivious to his wrestle of emotions. He smiled and shifted his gaze back to the highway. Maybe he could just fake a deep need for concentration, like he hadn't driven this exact road a dozen times before. Or dreamed about this exact scenario each night since Jackson had finally agreed to Jasper picking up the youngest Reilly from the airport. What was wrong with him? *Just talk, man.*

"So, uh, how was the flight?" Whoa. Master of scintillating conversation, right there. "I bet you're tired, huh?"

As if on cue she yawned, then laughed. "Sorry. It's not the company. Although maybe it is."

Her words shot daggers to his heart. He was boring?

"You're awfully quiet," she prodded. "Are you okay?"

"Yep. It's, uh, just been a busy time lately," he hedged. Busy wrangling his emotions back to where they should be. In the friend zone, or the neutral zone, which was where Ellie's professional hockey playing brother Mitchell had once warned him to stay.

He hadn't minded when Mitchell had first said that back in high school, but now, eight years on, he really wished for a do-over. And that Mitchell hadn't eyed him at Christmas when Ellie's scream of excitement had catapulted her into Jasper's arms, and he'd had to pretend he was glad about her going so far away. And yeah, he knew that made him sound selfish, and he was genuinely glad for her sake she'd finally get the chance to live her dream. But maybe he hadn't been quick enough to hide his dismay because he remembered Mitchell's narrowed gaze as if he knew what was tumbling around Jasper's heart.

Ugh. Enough of this introspection. He had to make her believe everything was okay. Which it *was*. He gritted his teeth.

"Sorry. I haven't slept well lately." Because he'd been imagining this very scenario. Well, not the one filled with awkwardness, but the one where she'd realize that she missed him like he'd missed her and never want to go away again. *Stop it!* "Anyway, tell me about your flights. Did everything go okay? You obviously made all your connections. Was the plane food terrible? What was the weather like when you left London?"

She laughed, a sound that trickled joy across his heart. He'd always loved her laugh. "Give me a second. You just went from Silent Man to Mr. Talkative in a heartbeat."

"Hey, I'm interested." Too interested. He glanced across. Did she hear the loaded nature of that statement?

"I know." She patted his hand, resting near the console, and he swerved.

"Sorry," he muttered.

"These roads are icy," she said.

Yeah, it wasn't ice that had caused his overcorrection. Try the sparks her fingers held.

And that was exactly why he had to be careful. He couldn't let her know that he liked her, and yet he couldn't go too far the other way and make her think he didn't care. He had to somehow find the happy medium, and be careful not to over-steer his interactions with her and make his emotions plain. He ground his teeth. All this second guessing meant he'd be single-handedly paying for the dentist's next vacation to Mexico. "So, you gonna tell me or be a mystery?"

"Says the man who barely talked to me while I was away."

He peeked across. Her head had tilted.

"What was that about?"

He shrugged. How to admit that seeing her living her best life carved a giant hole in his heart. Because obviously if she was living her best life she didn't need him around. And just as he was bad at pretending now, he'd been bad at pretending then. "I, uh, have been busy with work," he hedged.

"Yeah, Jackson mentioned something about your dad. What happened? Was he unwell?"

"He had some minor health challenges," he said, as they drove alongside Lake Wallula. "But he's okay now."

"What was it?" she asked, as straight to the point as ever.

"Just some heart congestion."

"What? Like a heart attack?"

"Pains, but the doc has given him some medication, so he should be okay. I've picked up extra shifts at work."

"Wow. Well, no wonder you couldn't talk to me much. That's awful. I'm so sorry."

He lifted a shoulder, eyes on the road.

"You must've thought I was so self-centered, wanting to talk about my trip all the time," she said softly. "I'm sorry I didn't try harder."

Truth was she *had* tried, and it was him, jealous him, who hadn't wanted to see her, hadn't known how to deal with his stupid emotions. But he couldn't admit that, so could only say, "I don't think that's self-centered at all."

She placed her hand in his. He flinched, then grasped her fingers in a gentle squeeze before letting go, moving to hold the steering wheel. Nope. Holding her hand was not helpful to getting his emotions under control.

"So." He coughed to clear unwanted gruffness. "That's about all I've got. Now tell me about you. Your flights, the food, your trip, the highlights, lowlights, favorite places, people you met. I want to know everything." That's what a best friend would ask, right?

She shifted to settle against the car door, and sighed happily. Then proceeded to fill the next half hour with tales of ancient places, delicious food, and interesting people she'd encountered. Names slid past his ears: Paris, Rome, Corinth, Gallipoli, Pamplona, Sebastian, Edinburgh, Chatsworth, Highclere. Some he recognized, like Gallipoli. He was pretty sure he'd once heard Marianne Kennedy talking about the Gallipoli battlefields in her history classes at high school. But most descriptions he nodded along as he fought the whirl of emotions. Much to his shame he didn't hear some things, too busy doing his best to seem interested, like the friend he was supposed to be. *God, forgive me.*

"Oh, Jasper, it was just the *best* time." She gave another sigh of happiness. "I never knew how much I was missing out on, you know? I mean, don't get me wrong. I love Trinity Lakes but it was just so good to escape and realize just how big the world can be. And then to see all these amazing places I've only ever seen in books or on TV. I don't know, it made me feel special, and not just boring me."

"But you are special."

She snorted. "Anyway, I can't wait to go back again."

He swallowed a thick lump of something that was flavored with protest. "I'm glad you enjoyed yourself. But it's really good to have you home."

"Yeah."

He swiveled a look at her. "You don't want to be here?"

She shook her head. "I know this will sound so awful, but I can trust you, right?"

He pressed his lips together, and nodded, even as his heart shouted, *Nope, you can't.*

"I'm so grateful for the chance to have traveled, but I don't know what I'm going to do here now." She exhaled heavily. "I just want to go back, work in a museum in England somewhere, or go on an archeological dig. Trinity Lakes seems so boring by comparison."

Of course, she had to say that, just as they neared the sign welcoming visitors to their community. Poplars lined either side of the road as the large 'Welcome to Trinity Lakes' sign flashed past. He drove down Main Street, with its quirky stores and quaint lamps, then past the park with the obelisk commemorating fallen soldiers. Beyond lay the blue glint of Lake Wainscott, the green hills nearby holding gnarled grapevines. How could she not love it here? Sure, it might not have castles, but this had to be as pretty as any place in Switzerland or France.

"But don't tell anyone that, okay?" she said.

"Sure."

His chest tightened, her words sinking deeper within his heart. He had to stifle his emotions, stifle this stupid attraction. What was wrong with him that he couldn't be the friend she needed, could only dream of what could never be? How selfish did that make him?

He drove across the bridge, past the fun park, closed until summer, then up the hill to where a sign announced Trinity Lakes Bible College, where Lexi Franklin lived with her parents who ran the place. He took a right, following the road past the college, as a bolt of envy streaked through his heart. Jackson and Lexi were engaged and super happy in their little bubble of romance. His fingers gripped the wheel. Lexi had wanted to return to Trinity Lakes, but Ellie had made it clear that her preference for a future wasn't here.

Which meant seeking anything more than friendship was out of the question.

Which meant ensuring she'd never know the depths of his confusing feelings toward her.

Which probably meant doing his level best to avoid her.

*God, help me.*

CHAPTER TWO

"Oh, I'm so tired." Ellie yawned and stretched her arms above her head.

"I believe that's called jet lag." Jackson glanced up from his lunch. "Good morning. Or is it afternoon? Well, look at that. It's nearly one."

"What day is it?"

"Wednesday. You've been in bed for sixteen hours, Sleeping Beauty."

She plucked a grape from the bowl and threw it at him.

He caught it and popped it in his mouth. "Thanks."

She rolled her eyes at him and switched on the electric kettle. Since visiting England and Scotland she had a new appreciation for tea. The proper stuff. Like the pack of English Breakfast tea-leaves she'd bought at the place where they'd filmed the *Pride and Prejudice* movie. Hot tea, that used a teapot and everything.

"How is the ranch doing?" she asked, pivoting to face her brother. "Really."

Jackson shrugged, swallowing the rest of his mouthful of sandwich. "It's going better. I meant what I said before. Since

Cooper has taken more of an interest in the finances, and the Darcys have rented those fields, we're heading in the right direction."

"God bless Liam, huh?"

Liam Darcy, their multi-millionaire neighbor, whose interest in sustainability had led to a desire to expand his experimental solar farm from the Darcy ranch to the adjoining Reilly spread.

"God bless all the Darcys." Jackson pushed his plate away. "Hey, that reminds me, Olivia Darcy was asking about you at church the other day."

"Really?" They might be neighbors, but Ellie could count on one hand the number of times the elderly matriarch of the Darcy family had sought Ellie out for conversation.

"Yeah. I don't know what it's about, but hey, you've now got a heads up for when you next see her."

Which would likely be at church, in four days. "Good to know. Thanks."

"So, what are you going to do with yourself now you're back in the real world."

"What do you mean?" she asked, pouring the just-boiled water into the silver teapot. "I'm just gonna do what I've always done, I suppose. Cook and help out around the ranch."

"Yeah, about that." Jackson leaned back in his wooden chair. "You know Mom has been doing a lot better."

"Yeah—where is she by the way?"

"In Trinity Lakes, at a Bible study with Pastor Ladan's wife."

"Really?"

He nodded slowly. "Mom is like a different woman since Lexi came here."

Of course. She fought a smile. She'd noticed the number of times Lexi's name came up in conversation with Jackson since Ellie's arrival home yesterday afternoon. And yes, Lexi's nursing skills had seen Mom's health improve to pre-burnout stage. And while she appreciated this, and that Lexi was one of Ellie's best friends, that didn't mean she was immune from tease. "And who was the one who had to convince you to have Lexi come help Mom?"

"You did." He checked out the ceiling while releasing a mock sigh.

"So, how are things going with your new fiancée?"

He smiled. "Awesome."

"You got a wedding date yet?"

"Seriously? Did you forget that you asked us that last night?"

Oh, right. At her surprise welcome home dinner, where her family and friends had made her feel so special, and she'd regaled them all with hilarious tales from her time away. Jasper, she'd noticed, had left early, apologizing that he had an early start the next day. Given his trying family circumstances—she knew only too well the challenges of an unwell parent—she'd let him go with just an awkward, too-quick hug at the door. She'd noticed how he stiffened and that his gaze didn't quite meet hers. Maybe he'd just had a long day. And given his dad's recent health scare she guessed Jasper had been working extra hard at the Cohen's hardware store.

"Hey, how is Jasper's dad doing?" she asked.

Jackson shrugged, finishing the last of his sandwich. "He seems okay. We see him at the hardware and at church too, but I know Jasper's working harder so his dad can take it easy."

"Wow. And yet he came and collected me."

Her brother's chair scraped as he pushed to his feet. "He insisted." His dark gaze swept up to hers, his eyebrows lifting. "Something I need to know?"

"Nope." She retrieved one of her new Paris mugs from the counter, watching as the Eiffel Tower slowly lit up as she poured in the freshly brewed tea. Some might call her mug tacky, but she loved it.

"Eloise?"

"What?" She straightened, meeting his gaze. "There's nothing to tell. He was a bit weird, actually."

Jackson's brow puckered. "What do you mean?"

"He barely talked. Then he seemed to barely listen."

"Really? I thought—" Jackson's lips clamped, but a quirk on one side of his mouth made his thoughts plain.

"Yeah, well, you're wrong." Apart from that too-long hug Jasper had seemed really distant. Although she couldn't blame him. Not with everything else going on in his world.

"If you say so." Jackson palms-upped her.

Clearly her brother thought everyone was supposed to be in love. "Anyway, back to important things. What do you want me to do around the place?"

"Around the ranch?" He took his plate to the sink, brushed the crumbs into the bucket labeled 'Compost', then loaded his plate into the dishwasher.

Huh. Apparently Lexi had trained her brother to a new domesticated status. Maybe seeing her training bear fruit had been what had got her to say yes. "Yes, Jackson. Around the ranch. Is Mom cooking yet?"

"She's been cooking for months, Ellie. Sorry, sis, but that job ain't yours."

"Good. I'm no Nigella Lawson."

"Who?"

"Never mind." Trying to educate her brother about a certain English chef known as a domestic goddess was a waste of time. "So, you're not telling me any specific job, so I guess that means I get to be a lady of leisure. Woohoo! Well, in that case, now I've got my cup of tea, I'll go find a hammock and a book and a slave to peel me some grapes, and—"

"Not so fast. You can come riding with me."

"Ooh, no business bookkeeping work for you today?"

Jackson sighed. "Cooper has put all the bookkeeping online, and he basically does most of it these days."

"Really? Our tech-head brother is playing boss?"

"No." Jackson bristled. "He's just keeping an eye on things. It's helped."

She pressed her lips together as Fido came in for a head scratch. Last year, during one of their many family conferences, Cooper had mentioned to her and the brothers that Jackson hadn't taken a wage in years. Maybe it had been that realization that had seen them send her to Europe in compensation for the wages she'd never received either. Which begged the question… "So, um, are you getting paid now?"

He nodded. "I had to. Cooper's arranged things so there's enough for a basic wage for me, which really helps with getting married later this year."

"Oh, so you have picked a date. Sorry, there's been a lot going on and I can't remember everything that got said recently."

"Sometime before Christmas, Lexi said, because she'll have her first year of nursing at the hospital done. But nothing is pinned down." His gaze grew serious. "So yeah, Cooper has arranged things so the ranch can afford to now pay me. But…" He winced, his brown eyes holding apology.

Her heart grew tight. "But it still can't afford to pay me. Is that what you're saying?"

"When we start getting paying guests for the farm stay—the ranch stay—in summer there might be more cash to play with, but not until then. I'm sorry, Ellie. But you know I've always thought you should be aiming for more than this."

More than life on the ranch? She glanced away, unable to cope with the compassion on his face, uncertain exactly how she should feel. The huge red barn loomed through the kitchen window, the site of a New Year's dance fifteen months ago which had seen Liam Darcy meet his wife-to-be, Elissa Bennett. Last New Year's Eve had apparently seen all kinds of tourists downtown for the town celebrations, but she'd missed that, being on a plane already. Apparently flying on New Year's Eve meant tickets were cheaper.

But why was she feeling a little lost when this was exactly what she'd said to Jasper, that she hadn't wanted to get stuck in Trinity Lakes? It was weird. Except there was a world of difference between choosing to live and work elsewhere, and being told that was what would likely have to happen.

"Hey, don't look like that." He pulled her in for a hug. Another thing that had changed since the arrival of Lexi. Jackson was more affectionate these days.

"Well, that's easy for you to say." She drew back. "But just what am I going to do?"

He studied her as her words echoed around the room. For all she might have wanted to return to Europe it wasn't like she had the money to make it happen.

Panic streaked through her stomach. "I don't have a job, or any real qualifications." There'd never been enough money for college. But pointing this out now seemed fruitless. Especially with Jackson biting his bottom lip, like he had regrets too. "So what am I going to do?" she demanded.

"You can keep working here—"

"Gee, thanks."

"Come on, Ellie. What do you want me to say? To be honest, I kinda thought you'd want to extend your stay and find some fancy European museum to volunteer at."

"I did. But somehow even those kinds of jobs still require qualifications I don't have." She softened the edge in her tone with a tight smile.

His shoulders slumped. "I'm sorry there was never enough money for school."

"I know." Her heart sorrowed. "And I don't mean to sound like a brat, or that I'm ungrateful, especially when you all were so generous in sending me off on a dream vacation. It's just that

I've always assumed I would work at the ranch and now I just don't know what to do."

"You can still work here," he assured. "It's just good to keep your options open."

"Yeah? What options?"

"You could get married."

"This isn't last century, Jackson. I don't believe I need a man to complete me."

"Hey, nobody's saying that. I'm just saying there are guys out there who'd probably love to marry you."

"Name one."

"Jasper."

Her pulse quickened. "Don't be stupid. He's my friend." Who'd barely talked to her yesterday. Had time apart proved the opposite of that old saying, so instead of absence making hearts fonder it had proved they didn't really need each other? Guilt panged. She still couldn't believe she hadn't known about Mr. Cohen's ill health. Sure, she'd had a lot going on, but did her lack of knowledge suggest self-absorption? If so, maybe their friendship was a lot weaker than she'd realized, and they were nothing more than people brought together by location and convenience. Her heart wrenched. No, thinking like that was dumb. She and Jasper were cool. Or they soon would be. She'd just treat him like she always had. Her friend, her confidante, the one who stood by her side when all her brothers ganged up on her.

"Anyway, I really hope you're not suggesting I go off and marry some poor guy just so I can afford to study. That'd be completely lame."

He blew out a breath. "I'm not saying you should. But maybe you could talk to Lexi and her parents. They probably know about scholarships. I bet Liam Darcy does too."

Not that the area's richest man would ever need it. "Have you spoken to him recently?"

"You want me to ask him to fund you—?"

"Don't be daft." Another excellent word she'd come across while in England. It sounded softer than saying stupid, anyway.

"Look, I know there's a lot to get your head around, coming back here, trying to figure out the future, your job, and all that," Jackson said softly, "but it's not like you're in this on your own."

"It's fine Jackson. I know you and Mom will be happy to have me here."

"Yeah, that's not what I meant."

"Then what did you mean?"

"God, Ellie. God is with you, every step of the way, every moment of every day. Trust Him with your future, okay?"

"Sure." She withheld her eye-roll until Jackson's back turned. Sure, she believed in God, she attended church. Or at least she had in Trinity Lakes. Somehow her travels had seen her traveling a little too much on Sundays when she was away, or visiting grand cathedrals, whose services she could barely understand, seeing they were in French or German or Greek, or sometimes even Latin. But the ambiance and choral music had lifted her heart to God. Even if He felt far away now.

But her brother was right, and she could—should—trust God. The podcast she used as a sermon when she'd missed last Sunday's service drew back to mind. God could—would—direct her paths. She just needed to trust Him.

Jackson nodded. "Meet you in the barn."

"Yeah." She forced a smile which dropped away upon his exit outside. Then clasped the edge of the counter, as the Eiffel Tower lit up the side of her cup. "Hey God, I know it's been a while. But I really could do with some help in figuring out what to do."

———

"AND THAT'LL BE $24.99." Jasper smiled at Dean Wilder.

The pastor of Trinity Lakes Community Church pulled out his wallet and laid two twenties on the hardware counter. "Thanks Jasper."

"Thank you." He smiled and made change, grateful for the patrons who shopped local, instead of supporting larger businesses like Home Depot in Walla Walla, or Lowe's in Kennewick.

He moved from the counter, nodding to Jordan Andersson, working the other cash register. The place had been busier lately, with this weekend's Easter break meaning people had been sprucing up their homes for family visits. Jasper didn't do too much cashier work these days. Not since he'd taken on most of his dad's office work. And while there were people trained to work the front of house there weren't any others who could do that. So he slaved away, day after day, matching figures and ordering stock, then reporting back to his dad about daily earnings. A new housing development had seen more builders and tradesmen frequenting Cohen's Hardware in recent months. He was grateful, but knew he couldn't rely on such things. It didn't take much for a housing boom to go bust. What counted was ensuring the locals returned, which meant excellent customer service and initiatives to get people through the door. So, with his father's blessing, he'd started doing some Saturday do-it-yourself workshops, asking friends like Joel Manning, a local tiler, to demonstrate the best way to lay tile. He'd promoted the DIY course to Joel not as a way to do himself out of a job, but as a way to ensure they'd know who to turn to when their efforts went bad. Which, let's face it, most people doing DIY needed a redo from the professionals. And this way they'd know who to call to get the job done right.

He stopped to straighten a display of paint cans. Sure they might be about professional products for tradesmen, but it helped if things were attractively organized. He overheard a man's voice holding a slight Australian drawl asking Jordan whether they stocked specialist paint. A glance behind showed it was Peter Franklin, Lexi's dad, and director of the Trinity Lakes Bible College.

"Hey, Mr. Franklin," he said, holding out his hand.

"It's Peter, Jasper." He shook it. "How's your dad doing?"

"Much the same. Trying his best to take things easy."

"Tell him he's in our prayers."

"Yes, sir."

Jasper helped him with finding paint for a refresh of some classrooms. The staff at the Bible college were pretty hands on when it came to fixing things around the place, and often came in. After helping him, and once more thanking him for his prayers, Jasper moved back to the office and his computer where a long list of emails requiring attention reminded him of when he'd helped Jackson with his banking proposal last year. Of course, thoughts about the Reilly ranch quickly led to thoughts about Ellie, which led to thoughts about her future, and whether she'd ever consider him as more than just a friend. Which only showed the levels of his desperation and particular brand of pathetic and his need to focus on his job. Anyway, he could catch up with Jackson and do his best to subtly learn what he could at the basketball game tonight.

———

THE SQUEAK of sneakers and smack of ball on the high school basketball court hurried Jasper to the bleachers. He was late. He lifted a hand to Jackson, Matt Kennedy, Brandon Taylor, Logan Wylde, and Josh Ladan as they passed the ball to each other. He shrugged out of his heavy jacket and unzipped the sides of his track pants to reveal his shorts. Call him a wuss but driving from home to here in shorts felt too cold, thanks to last week's unseasonal low which had brought an unwelcome heavy dump of early spring snow.

"Late again." Brandon smirked.

"Everything okay?" Jackson asked, breathing heavily. Obviously he'd been here longer than the official meet up time of 7pm.

"Yeah. Just had to catch the folks up with the business."

"Here." Matt threw the ball at him.

He snatched it, and they played some three-on-three, the fast pace and banter good to clear the head and work out the kinks from a day spent sitting down too long in front of a computer. Half an hour later he was dripping with sweat, but knew a glow of satisfaction at having top scored again. He'd never achieved the athletic feats of Jackson's brother, NHL star Mitchell Reilly, or even Jackson himself, who'd been the wrestling champ of Trinity Lakes High. But despite not being as tall as some he'd always had a good eye and could sink a three-point basket better than most.

After Matt, Brandon, Logan, and Josh left he caught up with Jackson at Joe's Diner, where they ordered chocolate milkshakes and curly fries, fully loaded. Fitting rewards considering the workout they'd just endured.

Jackson slurped his shake, shoved in a cheese-and-bacon-smothered fry then leaned back against the booth. "Man, I needed that."

"Rough day?"

"Just the usual. Which is why it was good to work off some of the stress with exercise."

"It's not quite the same as wrangling bulls, huh?"

"Nope." Jackson's brow puckered. "Brutus is a stubborn dude, but he's a lot happier now."

Jasper remembered some drama about the bull last summer, whose efforts at siring had been thwarted temporarily by an infection diagnosed by the local vet, Jessica Martin. The Reillys had been thankful when that had cleared up, and Brutus had gone on to be the stud bull for a lot of ranches around these parts.

But Jackson still wore a frown. "What's wrong?"

Jackson's gaze slid up to meet Jasper's. "That sister of mine."

Jasper's heart kicked. "What's wrong with her?"

His lips rolled together, like he wasn't sure whether to spill the beans.

"Fine. Don't tell me."

Jackson exhaled, rubbed his forehead. "That's just it. I don't know. I know she's only been back a couple of days now, but she seems a little off."

"Off? How?"

"You know that Ellie has always loved the ranch, and the animals. Well, she's not the same. It's like she's all confused about the future. Doesn't know whether she's coming or going. Did she say anything to you on the trip back from the airport about wanting to return to Europe?"

"What?"

Jackson's eyebrows pushed up. "So she didn't?"

"I didn't think she meant it," he admitted.

"So she did. Huh."

"Hey, I'm sure she'll get over it." She had to. She had to want to stay. *Please God.*

Jackson studied him, his brow lowered. "So there's nothing between you two?"

"Nope." He glanced away. He was too tired to deal with Jackson's protective big brother act tonight.

"I just thought the way you insisted on collecting her from the airport meant you wanted there to be."

"Even if I did, there's not much point if she's wanting to move away."

"So you do."

"I didn't say that."

"You didn't have to. Wow."

Jasper fought the urge to fidget as Jackson's gaze lay heavy on him. "What? Have you got some objection? You didn't say anything the other day about having a problem with me."

"I don't have a problem with you. It's just—" He clamped his mouth shut.

"Just what?" Jasper pressed.

"It's just hard to rely on her with any certainty at the moment. And I wouldn't want to see you counting on something that might not work out."

"I'm not counting on her," he insisted. "We're friends, that's all. And anyway, she's probably just got a lot to think about right now. It'd be hard enough adjusting to normal time zones again after being so far away, let alone having to focus on regular work, instead of traveling and doing what she wanted when she wanted."

Jackson exhaled. "I know. But that's the other thing. She might need to start looking for work someplace else."

"What?" Where could she go? He couldn't have her leave. Would his secret plan ever get a chance to succeed? "I thought the ranch had enough going on to keep her busy."

"But still not enough to pay her. You've seen the books." Last year when Jasper had helped Jackson try to win a bank business loan. "You know things have been tight. I feel like I've let her down by not providing her with an education."

"Not everybody needs a college education," he protested. "Besides, you're her brother, not her father. That should've been his role."

Jackson's face tightened as it did every time his father was mentioned. Jasper had heard various versions of the story over the years. Donald Reilly had disappeared over two decades ago, had just walked out and left his family, and had since been legally declared dead. Jackson had power of attorney and could make decisions concerning the ranch. But any mention of the missing Reilly was a sore point.

"Ellie is tough, and she'll figure out what to do," Jasper assured. "You don't need to worry about her."

Her brother studied him then nodded. "Pray for her?"

"Already do."

"Huh. Should've known," Jackson muttered.

"It's what friends do."

"Friends, huh?"

"Friends," he said firmly. And further confirmation that he should do his best to keep away.

Because he couldn't risk pushing for more when she was going to break his heart.

CHAPTER THREE

Saturdays. Was there any better day in the week than a Saturday? Especially when it was the Saturday sandwiched between Good Friday and Easter Sunday, and chocolate bunnies were in abundance, one awaiting her on her bed as soon as she finished this delightful chore.

Ugh. She grasped the pitchfork more securely and continued hefting out the mess lining the floor of Brutus's pen.

"Hey, watch it," Denny called from his position mere inches from where the contents had splattered.

"Sorry." She wrinkled her nose at the ranch foreman, then resumed mucking out the enclosure.

This. She sure hadn't missed this while in Europe. Maybe God thought she needed humbling because it felt kind of agonizing to go from the heights of cathedral grandeur to the lows of mucking out stalls.

Denny, Miguel and the other workers hadn't exactly been shy about their tease in recent days, pointing out the contrast between her job now—one she used to do as second nature—and what they called the globetrotting lifestyles of the rich and famous.

Hardly. She was neither rich nor famous. But knowing that protesting would only earn her more teasing she kept her mouth shut, even as she wondered how long it would take before she settled back into the ranch's life of sweat and hard work.

Her mind drifted, back to the fabulous sights and places she'd seen. Had da Vinci even dreamed of mundane things or had his life been all artistry and magic? Had Claude Monet ever wished to make candles or be a wheelwright, or had his passion for color and creativity consumed his life? She'd seen Pompeii's ruins and knew its residents were ordinary folk, but somehow even their lives seemed elevated when preserved in ash and rock. Her life, by contrast, seemed so ordinary and boring. Dull as dishwater. And while she knew slaves two thousand years ago must've mucked out stalls not dissimilar to this one, it felt a world away.

Irritation bubbled, low, persistent, something she loathed to acknowledge. She *was* grateful to have had such an amazing experience many wished for and few had. Really, she was. But contentment seemed so far away. Yes, she knew about jet lag, and had even heard about reverse culture shock, and the pangs of reassimilating after time spent overseas. But it didn't feel like she'd been wearing rose-colored glasses in Europe. Instead it felt like she'd had the blinders taken off, and instead of only seeing straight ahead she'd seen how wide and vast the world could truly be.

And now she was back, almost like her adventure hadn't even happened, like everyone expected her to be the same when she felt so different. *The world is bigger than Trinity Lakes, with so many interesting people in it*, she longed to say. But saying so wasn't going to help anyone. Which left her feeling discontented, slightly disgruntled, and tired of so many things.

So many things felt the same, but also different. Even time with her mother felt strange and new. The past few years had seen the weight of responsibility lead to Mom's slow decline and increased time in bed. To see her now, almost back to normal, bright and cheerful, her efforts in the house so much more energetic than when Ellie had left three months ago, was another shock to the system.

It was like Ellie didn't fit here anymore. Jackson's comments about the ranch not being able to pay her had only made that clearer. So where was she supposed to be? In some ways she almost wished things were the way they'd been a year ago. But she hardly dared articulate that—for how could any loving daughter not be one hundred percent glad her mom was back and contributing again? Even daring to think along those lines made her hate herself. How self-centered was Ellie that she only thought about how this affected her and her future? But things *had* changed. The ranch had changed. People had changed. Mom had. Jackson had. Even Jasper had.

Her spirits plunged deeper. He still hadn't called, which was obvious proof she must've just read too much into that long hug and look he'd leveled her at the airport. What kind of idiot was she? She really was losing the plot by imagining things like that.

She finished and moved back through the slush-covered yard to the house, Fido whining at her feet. She'd now really earned that chocolate bunny. And maybe a couple of those windmill cookies Mom had started buying again.

She slid open the glass door and sniffed appreciatively. "Something smells good."

Her mom smiled. "I'm just prepping for lunch tomorrow. Your brother called and he's coming tonight."

"Coop is coming?" She knew that Mitchell had hockey games scheduled either side of Easter Sunday. Dermott's Greener Gardens business meant he rarely left the Independence Islands.

"Yes. He's flying into Tri-Cities and will hire a car and get in late tonight. So we'll all attend the Easter service together. Won't that be good?"

"Absolutely."

"So I'm just making sure we have things ready for when we get back."

Ellie nodded. "Need some help?"

"Thanks for asking, but I've got everything under control."

Ellie wrapped an arm around her mom's shoulders and gave her a gentle squeeze. "It's so good to see you back to momming again," she murmured.

"It's so good to have the energy to feel like I can," her mother said, patting Ellie's hand. "How are you doing?"

"Just dandy."

Her mother shifted, eyeing her with a serious look. "It'll take some time but you'll soon feel settled again."

Ellie nodded, biting back her protest. She didn't want to settle. Settling felt like less than. Lower than. Like a tree digging in its roots and becoming impossible to move. And a stubborn hope within still clung to a desire to have more, to see more, to *be* more than just a rancher's daughter on a small ranch in a forgotten corner of the state.

But what if this was all God had for her? Panic rose, and she sucked in a deep breath to tamp it down. Jackson's words the other day rang softly at the back of her mind. God was still with her, every moment, every day. Even when she didn't want to be here. She gritted her teeth. Which meant good daughter vibes had better start showing up. Even if she only felt like they'd show up by her speaking them into existence. "So, um, are you sure there's nothing I can do? You don't need any extra help around the house?"

"I'm fine, Ellie. You should ask Jackson."

She nodded, reserving her protest behind her lips. Jackson didn't seem to need her either, especially with Cooper's efforts having lifted much of the business weight of the ranch off his shoulders, leaving him more time to focus on the ranch. It was like Ellie's existence here was pointless. If only there was a way to escape to Europe again. See Sebastian again. Feel alive and special again.

The phone rang. "Can you get that?" her mom asked, her hands covered in flour.

"Sure." She hurried to the landline in Jackson's slightly less-messy-than-she-remembered office. Look at her: reduced to secretary status. She snatched up the phone. "Hello?"

"Is this the number for the Reilly ranch?"

"Yes. Can I help you?"

"I hope so. I understand you have ranch stays."

"That's correct." One of Lexi's initiatives that had led to a flurry of Bible College students repainting the bunkhouse accommodation for free last August as part of their contributions to serving their local community. There were still some tweaks Jackson was insisting on, but he'd said they'd start advertising soon. Any business was better than none. Ranches couldn't just depend on cows these days.

"Excellent. I was speaking to my friend Mindy and she mentioned a beautiful ranch I simply had to stay at. I saw her pictures on Instagram. It looks simply divine."

Ellie blinked. Her sister-in-law Mindy, Dermott's wife, had already started advertising? Still, Ellie couldn't admit she was unaware. That wasn't the way to come across as professional. "It is a very pretty area, yes."

"Well, I'd like to book accommodation please."

"Oh! Uh, sure. Please hold the line a moment while I check our availability."

She covered the phone and moved to the wall calendar with its months crossed out for accommodation. According to this, Jackson hadn't wanted to start until summer. She studied the schedule. "And may I ask when you were thinking?"

"Are you open mid-April?"

In two weeks? Jackson had a big red line through that date, but what was the point in having accommodation ready and waiting without anyone staying in it? Especially when she was here, at loose ends, needing something to do. And having paying guests come to stay would help get the ranch's coffers in better shape. "I think we can make that work."

"Oh, wonderful!"

As Ellie wrote down details she learned that the woman was planning to visit Spokane for a family wedding but wanted a place for a quality family vacation before heading back to the hectic life of New York. Further conversation led to a quick scroll through Insta which showed Mindy hadn't advertised the ranch stay, but had recently posted some throwback pics of the ranch from their last visit here. Apparently the photos of golden hills and horses had done the selling, one thing leading to another so that Marcie had insisted on knowing where Mindy had stayed, which had led to today's call.

"Well, we look forward to welcoming you here in two weeks."

"Thanks so much. We can't wait."

She'd just ended the call when Jackson entered the room. He nodded to the phone. "Who was that?"

She beamed. "Our first booking."

"For the ranch stay?"

"Yep." She moved to the wall, scrawled the dates on the calendar.

"But that's April. We weren't going to open until June."

"But we now have a booking for April, so we're going to say yes. Marcie and her family of four are coming for five days."

"How'd she even know we were doing this?"

"Mindy posted a pic of the ranch on Instagram."

"Wow." He shook his head. "But we haven't even finalized the website and online booking system."

"Looks like that's something you can ask Mindy to hurry up

and finish." Her sister-in-law had excellent social media skills, and last year had volunteered to update the Reilly Ranch website with the new accommodation details. "Anyway, it's money, right? You should be glad for more cash."

He eyed her. "And you're going to be running the ranch stays now, are you?"

"Got nothing else to do."

He sighed. "Don't be like that. You know we want your help. We need your help, Ellie."

"So let me help," she said. "I want to do this."

"You've already told the woman yes, so I guess we have to make it happen."

"I guess we do." She placed her hands on her hips. "Honestly Jackson, I don't understand why you wouldn't open it earlier. What's the point of delaying?"

"Because we needed someone to take responsibility for it. It's not just answering a phone and taking bookings. It's preparing breakfast baskets, and changing sheets, and leading people on tours. You know I'm going to be too busy to do too much of that."

"Well, hello. What am I? Chopped liver?"

"Look, we wanted to give you time to readjust to life here, and didn't want you to feel pressured into doing something you didn't want to do."

"Didn't want—? We talked about this last year, Jackson. I even talked to Tabby about how to run things. I was fine then, and I'm still fine to do it now. Come on."

He arched an eyebrow but didn't say anything. Which left her wondering what he wasn't saying. So she raised her own.

"*Are* you fine?" he asked.

Well, there was no need to wonder anymore. "Yes," she snapped.

"You don't exactly sound like it. I know it'll take some time to settle back in. But we're a team, Ellie. You know that."

It sure didn't feel like one. She felt sidelined. Less valued. And what was with everyone telling her she'd soon feel settled again? Just how bratty had she appeared?

"Do you want to go back to Europe, is that it?"

She heaved out a sigh and moved to the window, folding her arms as she looked out to the big pines out the front, the dark green sentinels along the muddied drive exactly as she'd always known. Would saying yes make her sound like a spoiled brat? How could she say that when her family had sacrificed so much for her already?

"Okay, don't hate me, but I just feel so confused," she confessed. "Yes, part of me wants to return to Europe, and so I'm finding it hard to get back into the swing of ordinary things here. But you know I love the ranch and you and Mom and everything here, so I'm torn. I'm sorry I'm being a pain."

"You're not being a pain. Just honest and real."

"Too honest, I bet."

He shook his head. "I just want you to be happy. And I can understand that it's hard to come down from the highs of your adventures in Europe to ordinary life again."

She bit her lip, hating the fact the backs of her eyes were beginning to burn with unshed tears. Look at her. Where had tough Ellie gone? Maybe she'd left her behind in London. Or maybe it was simply her tiredness that was making her emotional. "I just feel unsettled, like I'm not really where I'm meant to be anymore. For as long as I can remember I felt like this is what I'm meant to do. But now it's like I've come home and I'm trying to pull on an old boot that doesn't fit anymore. And it's just so weird because I always thought I'd be here, just like you've always had the ranch, and Mitchell's had his hockey, and Dermott's had his plants. I thought ranch life is what I'm meant to do, but now I'm not so sure."

"What do you want to do?"

"Something with history." She blinked, the words had

popped out so fast she hadn't had to think. Yet it was true. After seeing so many historical treasures that *was* what she wanted to do.

But a job involving her passion for history felt as distant as a shooting star, impossible to grasp, forever out of reach. For how could she ever do something when she had no real skills or qualifications?

She fake-yawned, using the action to wipe at a few stubborn tears that had leaked, then turned to face her brother. "But hey, we all know beggars can't be choosers, right?"

"You're not a beggar, Ellie. Remember, you're God's child. He's a good Father who loves to bless His kids."

Unlike her real dad whom she didn't know at all. How could she when he'd left before she'd turned one? The only memories she had she was pretty sure had been introduced by family tales and folklore. And none of them were good.

"Well, God might be good, but I'd love to see how He can make something out of the impossible." Ugh. She hated the defeat in that phrase. She never used to be that person.

Jackson smiled. "Good thing that's His specialty. Hey, don't forget Olivia Darcy wants to speak to you. She'll probably do so after the service tomorrow."

Curiosity mounted. "You don't know what it's about?"

He shrugged. "She didn't say. But it might be exciting. Regardless, I'm praying for you, sis."

"Thanks."

Her phone vibrated with a notification and she dug it from her back pocket and glanced at the screen. Her eyes widened. Sebastian really did want to visit her? Her heart fluttered. He'd sent an email late last night, but while she'd mentioned it to her family, she hadn't realized he'd be this eager to see her. She smiled. Imagine how wonderful it would be to have part of the magic of Europe here in Trinity Lakes. To feel special and chosen once again. Maybe the upcoming weeks would be bearable after all.

———

JASPER STOLE A PEEK AT ELLIE, seated between her mom and Lexi, who sat next to Jackson. Ellie's lips kept pulling into a tiny smile, as if secretly pleased or amused by something. Jackson eyed him and Jasper returned his gaze to the front. The stained-glass windows displayed the risen Savior, most appropriate for this Resurrection Sunday.

Theo Ladan continued his sermon, the message to trust God to direct their paths seeming most pertinent today. How often did Jasper want to wander his own way, without heeding the wisdom of the Savior? Impatience sometimes seemed to be his middle name, and possibly Ellie's too, judging from the way she kept tapping her jeans-clad knees. That, and the way she kept smiling, made it look as if she was excited.

The pastor finished with a prayer, then, "And don't forget the last of our special healing meetings this weekend, which are a great opportunity to remember what our Lord has done. We know God is the only one who can truly heal. Doctors can treat symptoms but our Maker is the only one who understands our true needs and offers true healing. Please invite your friends, and pray for a continued movement of God's Spirit in hearts and lives, too."

Ellie's smile flashed, wider this time. Something was definitely up with her.

"What's going on with you?" he asked her later, when they were in the foyer.

"What do you mean?"

"You. You keep smiling. What's happened?"

"Nothing." Her lips curved for a fraction of a second.

"There. You just did it again."

"Can I help it if I'm happy? Isn't it what we all should be on Easter Sunday? Happy because of what our Lord and Savior has done for us?"

"Yes, but I haven't seen you look this happy on any other Easter Sunday before."

"Well, maybe this year I've got more things to be happy about."

"Yeah? Like what?" he challenged.

"Like I'm happy to hear people have been getting healed at the services. I'm happy about Mom being better, more finances, having been to Europe." Her smile flashed again.

"It's something to do with Europe isn't it?" At her nod his heart sank. "Am I supposed to guess? Come on, Ellie. You're not the type of girl to play games."

"Who says I'm playing games?"

"So why don't you just tell me?"

She shrugged. "You don't need to know all my business, Jasper."

Hurt creased his chest, and he nodded stiffly.

Something that looked like regret crossed her features, and she took a step toward him, opening her mouth as if to speak.

"Ah, here she is," Mrs. Darcy called to her. "Miss Eloise. Happy Easter to you, my dear."

"And to you, Mrs. Darcy."

"Hmm. I won't be the only Mrs. Darcy for long it seems."

"Have Liam and Elissa settled on a wedding date?" Ellie asked politely.

"Later in the Spring, or so I believe. Apparently Elissa's family needed to wait until the university semester break to come over again. I think they'll all be here. Even that dreadful youngest one." Olivia Darcy gave a delicate shudder.

Jasper bit back a smile. He'd seen—and heard about—some of the audacious exploits concerning Lydia Bennett.

"Anyway, that wasn't what I wanted to speak to you about.

Have you got a spare evening this week? You could bring your mother and brother too, if you wish." Her gaze shifted to Jasper. "And your young gentleman friend too, if you like."

"Oh, we're just friends," Ellie said.

Her words slashed heat across Jasper's chest which soon crept up his neck. Mrs. Darcy glanced at him questioningly, as if wondering why someone would quietly fund a job for someone who dismissed him as 'just' a friend. Then she gave a little shrug as if to say it didn't matter.

Except it did matter. He didn't like how much it mattered. And he really didn't like how Ellie was keeping secrets from him. Best friends didn't do that, did they?

"I'll leave you to it," he said. Clearly these conversation bubbles didn't include him. "Happy Easter, Mrs. Darcy."

"And to you, young man."

He nodded. Yeah, he'd been pretty sure she didn't remember his name, and that just seemed to confirm it. He glanced at Ellie, but she was intently focused on whatever the older woman was saying, and didn't see him leave.

His stomach dropped. He might as well be invisible for all the attention she paid him.

"Hey dude, why do you look like you've just lost your best friend?" Cooper Reilly, Jackson's younger brother asked.

Because he was starting to feel like he had? Jasper shrugged. "When did you get into town?"

"Last night. I got a few days off and thought I'd fly up to see the family." Cooper's gaze drifted to Jessica Martin, the local vet.

"Uh huh." Apparently that wasn't all he'd come to see. "How is business?"

"Much the same. You?"

"Keeping busy."

Cooper's mouth curved in a wry expression so like Ellie's Jasper had to look away. Ellie was now talking to Jess's mom,

Shona Martin, and Georgia Darcy. He swallowed. Why did she look so animated when talking to everyone—except him?

"I heard you picked her up from the airport," Cooper said.

He instantly shifted his gaze back to face his friend. "Yeah. That's what friends do."

"*Some* friends."

Was that edge in Cooper's voice a brotherly warning? He shrugged, aiming for nonchalance as he stuck his hands in his back pockets. "This friend does, anyway."

He saw his parents, his dad being prayed for by some of the older men in church, including Pastor Ladan. He should probably go over and see how they were doing. And get away from the latest Reilly brother interrogation.

"Okay, whatever."

Whatever? So Cooper didn't believe him either? Note to self: never play poker. Apparently his friends could read him better than a book.

Cooper sighed. "I probably shouldn't be saying anything, but Ellie mentioned this morning that she got an email this week."

"Okay."

Cooper's gaze slammed into Jasper's. "It was from a French dude."

His chest tightened. He swallowed. "And?"

"And apparently he's planning to come out to see her."

"Okay." He cleared his throat to remove the squeak. Maybe that was what someone whose heart had just been ripped out sounded like. He forced himself to meet Cooper's eyes.

Cooper's full-of-pity eyes. "I'm sorry, man."

He needed to get out of here. This was pain. "What for? Like I said, we're just friends." He forced a smile. "Enjoy your day."

"You too."

Yeah, there was now a pretty solid chance that enjoyment wasn't going to happen today.

He moved away, but somehow Ellie's glance connected with

him. He couldn't find a smile for her. And when she moved toward him he knew a desperate desire to run. He couldn't see her, couldn't speak to her, couldn't touch her. He sure wasn't making that mistake again.

His chest felt like collapsing, and the only reason he kept breathing was because he had to keep up the pretense he was still functioning.

He swerved around Mrs. Ladan and her daughter Jodie, nodded to James Martin, all the while conscious he needed to escape. He could do that. He found a smile for Pastor Ladan, and said to his dad, "See you at home."

Even home felt too far away, as he hurried to his truck and gunned the engine, conscious the squeal of wheels hardly said subtle exit.

But he had to get away. Before everyone realized that he'd fooled himself into hoping for things that could never be. Would never be. For why would Ellie ever look at him? Not when she had apparently found herself a European boyfriend.

## CHAPTER FOUR

"Now my dear Eloise, would you like to try some gravy?"

"Thank you, Mrs. Darcy." Ellie accepted the delicate blue-and-white boat-shaped porcelain dish apparently designed for this one purpose. She added a trickle of delicious-smelling sauce to her roast chicken, and strove to remember her best manners appropriate for the finery surrounding her.

The Darcy dining room possessed two chandeliers, like something at Chatsworth, and the antique table and chairs seemed of that ilk too. She glanced across the formal table and managed a smile at her mother and Jackson, then another for Mrs. Darcy, seated at the head of the table.

"Please forgive the absence of my grandchildren," Olivia said. "Georgia and Elissa returned to Seattle for university studies earlier today, and Liam flew with them, as he has a meeting in Vancouver tomorrow." She gave a sniff. "Really, the way he carries on about Elissa one would think she wasn't capable or clever enough to complete a post-doctorate degree. But I suppose it won't take too long before those two get married and learn that marriage is not all romance and roses."

Okay. Ellie exchanged wide eyes with Jackson, who looked like he was trying not to laugh.

The evening had felt very strange, and the way Olivia Darcy had condescended to include Ellie in every conversation made her wonder just what she wanted. Still, a girl wasn't about to knock back an opportunity to dine with the Darcys. Invitations were rare, invitations from Olivia herself virtually unheard of, and a refusal might mean no more. And the fact she kept asking Ellie about her trip, her favorite museums and castles she visited, felt like an opportunity to grasp onto a dream that felt like it was slipping even further from her fingers. Had she really traveled or was it just a fantasy?

The meal progressed until finally Olivia placed her knife and fork in the center of her plate, and glanced down the table at Ellie. "I trust you enjoyed that?"

"Yes, indeed." Ellie pushed her finished plate away, lessening the temptation to wipe her finger to clean up the gravy residue. "Thank you."

"I appreciate your patience, but I, unlike my grandson, have never liked mixing business with pleasure. I thought we might discuss things then have dessert, if that suits you, Eloise."

"O-of course."

"Very well."

The Darcy's cook and housekeeper—Brenda—came in and cleared their plates, and the mood soon shifted again.

Ellie's stomach tensed, and for some reason she wished Jasper was here. He'd always known how to make her feel at ease. But since Sunday he'd not answered her calls or texts. She hoped that was caused by work and busyness, and not due to that strange moment following the Sunday service when he'd looked at her with such a defeated expression. She'd tried to follow, only to have Shona Martin stop her and welcome her back after her lengthy time away. Jasper was usually so good at instantly replying. But the distance that had grown in recent days seemed to be increasing, leaving a yawning chasm in her chest that not even the thrill of Sebastian's proposed visit could take away.

"Now, I have to admit I have enjoyed speaking with someone who appreciates the value of museums and the like." Olivia fiddled with her glasses as she peered at Eloise. "Remind me again, which was your favorite?"

"I loved the Louvre."

"Naturally."

"And the V & A in London."

"What's the V & A?" Jackson asked.

"The Victoria and Albert Museum. It has a huge collection of everything from jewelry to art to furniture and textiles, from different cultures, and different time periods. You name it, they've got it. It was awesome." She'd visited several times, and particularly loved the fashion through the ages exhibit, and the original 1700s gilt and mirrored room. She'd spent hours there and still hadn't seen everything.

"I agree. It is quite wonderful, isn't it?" Olivia said. "It does my heart good to see a young person who appreciates the value of understanding history. I find most young people these days tend to look at history only to point out our ancestor's sins, rather than seeing historical people and decisions as a product of their times."

Ellie nodded. "Like books that were written that now people want to update to be more politically correct."

"Simply ghastly. How can they not realize that one can never make better choices if we whitewash history to suit the cultural norms of the day? I truly believe it is far better to see, and then learn from, our mistakes." She folded her hands on the table. "But I suppose that leads me to my point. One doesn't want to repeat the sins of the past, and museums are supposed to display a full history, are they not? Which is what always disappointed me about the Trinity Lakes historical museum."

A tickle of excitement rolled through Ellie's heart. No. She wasn't about to say—

"I've had various people, like Marianne Kennedy, often suggest we should reopen it." Olivia studied Ellie.

She swallowed. "I think that would be awesome, but it'd take a lot of work. Hasn't it been closed for years?"

"Exactly. I'm afraid that ever since the passing of the previous director there has been no one with a passion for history to take it on. And there's little to no indigenous content, which obviously has to be included. One doesn't want to perpetuate the lie that nobody lived in these parts until white settlers came."

"Absolutely not."

"So," Olivia's head tilted. "I wonder where one might find a motivated younger person who loves history who might be interested in undertaking such a role?"

Ellie blinked. Was she seriously asking her to take on a job she'd dreamed about for years? But if she said yes, what would that mean for the ranch? For future travel? For potential studies?

"Eloise, I asked you here, and your mother and brother too, as I understood from a number of people that your heart has always been invested in our museum, and now, with your mother's health improved, it might be the perfect time to see if you have time free to devote to such a cause."

"I... I don't know what to say." She glanced at her mom. Jackson. Both looked as stunned as her, so clearly they hadn't known either. That made her feel slightly better. Jackson's hints about finding paid work away from the ranch hadn't been because he knew about this, then. The problem was, as enticing as this opportunity was, she still needed paid work. But how to ask such a thing... "I'm sorry, my mind is whirling. This is such a surprise to me. I've been thinking about my future direction, and I know I want to travel more, which means I'd, er, need a paying job."

Olivia smiled. "Naturally this would come with a generous stipend."

It would? "Forgive me, but how? The museum has been closed for years, and isn't generating income."

"Let's just say there is a board that is prepared to pay to ensure the right person gets the job."

"And you think that's me?"

"I know that's you."

Was Olivia Darcy a fairy godmother in disguise? Or simply an answer to prayer?

"I have long had a passion for the history of our area," Olivia continued, "and I have been waiting for the time when someone capable and equally passionate has had the time to devote to it. And I'm not getting any younger. Naturally, Marianne Kennedy has commitments with the school, and you could not take it on when your mother was unwell. But recently we received a not insubstantial donation to supply the wages for the position, so now, I truly feel this is the right timing. The right timing of the Lord, one might say."

Ellie shivered. This did feel like an answer to a prayer she'd hardly dared to pray.

"It's why I wanted your nearest and dearest present to hear my proposal in case they had objections, or need you at the ranch." Olivia glanced at Jackson and her mom.

"I want you to be happy, Ellie," Mom said.

"You know this is what you want to do," Jackson assured.

Well, it had been. Until Europe. "When are you wanting to reopen?"

"I had hoped the weekend just before Memorial Day. May twenty-fifth, I believe."

"But that's less than two months away."

"Something that a capable and energetic young woman would easily manage, I'm sure."

She winced. "But I do have some commitments. The ranch will be taking in some paying guests, and I have a friend coming to stay from Europe for a while." Her cheeks heated.

Olivia smiled. "Am I to infer from your blush that it is a male friend?"

Ellie nodded, feeling suddenly shy. "I met Sebastian at the Musee D'Orsay. He was a wonderful tour guide in Paris, and we met up again in London. He's coming in a few weeks."

"Well, I'm sure the role could accommodate such things. Especially if you were to start soon. So, is that a yes?"

"I beg your pardon, ma'am?"

"Does that mean you'll agree to do it? Run the museum, I mean. After you check the paperwork and stipend is suitable of course." She named a sum.

Ellie's jaw swung open. She closed it. "Um." She glanced at Jackson. He nodded gently. Maybe he was part hypnotist for she found herself nodding too. "I... I had never imagined—I don't know how long I'll be here."

"You'd be here long enough to get things started, I'm sure. Then, if you wished to pursue travel, or studies, or something else, the hard work of relaunching would be done."

"But are you sure you want me?" she asked Olivia. "I mean, I've been told I can be a little forthright sometimes."

"And that's exactly why we need you. You'd be relying on volunteers, and they need someone with a good head on their shoulders who can make things happen and not be a pushover."

"I'm sorry, but I just don't know what to say."

"Then I'll make it easy for you. Just say yes." Olivia's laughter tinkled.

Ellie's excitement kindled. "I can really do what I want?"

"Within reason. Naturally, you would need to discuss things with the board, but we're very eager to not delay as we'd like to be open for the summer. I think a good starting point would be to visit the museum and see what exhibits they have there already."

"You'd have to fit this around shifts at the ranch stay," Jackson reminded her.

"Of course." She wasn't about to let that go.

"And around visits from other friends, too." Jackson smirked.

Like Sebastian. Her heart fluttered again. She couldn't *wait* to see his handsome face again. He was so cultured and sophisticated, so fun to be with, so unlike everyone around here.

Her attention returned to Olivia. "You truly want someone like me, even though I'm not educated or trained in museum management?"

Olivia cleared her throat. "Your name was suggested to us."

It had been? God bless them. Who had believed in her so much? "Who?"

"I'm afraid I'm not at liberty to say. But the board has agreed we can offer the position to you. Marianne would also be ideal but has no wish to retire from teaching, and anyway, she's on the board so that would not suit." Olivia sighed. "I know it does sound like a lot of responsibility. And even though there would be a stipend to pay you for your time, and the flexibility to basically choose your own hours, I understand this job would not suit everyone."

"It suits her," Jackson said dryly.

"So is that a yes then, Eloise?"

"When would you need me to start?"

"As soon as possible. If you can spare the dear girl from her duties at the ranch, of course," Olivia said to Jackson and Mom.

"I think we can spare her." Jackson grinned at her. "Can't we?"

Was this for real? It still seemed so out-of-the-blue, so impossible, yet a once-wished-for dream come true. Ellie glanced at her mom who gave her an encouraging smile.

"Then okay." Ellie turned to Olivia. "Yes, please."

————

*KNOCK KNOCK.*

Jasper pushed back from the desk and glanced at the door. Then straightened.

"Hey stranger." Ellie's grin could light bonfires. "You got five minutes?"

He pushed a weary hand through his hair. Five minutes with Ellie could mean anything from fifteen minutes to five hours. But even though he was nursing battered hopes, it was like his mouth had forgotten, trained in the way of forever as he'd always been a sucker for her schemes. "Sure. What's up?"

"Come with me."

"Now?"

"It's almost closing time, right? You can come, can't you? You don't have Bible study or basketball with the guys or anything?"

Only a truckload of accounts to deal with. But they'd still be there tomorrow. "Five minutes?" he said, studying her, still hovering at the door.

"Okay, maybe ten." She flashed another grin that sparkled light through the darkness shrouding his heart. "I had to come and ask in person, seeing as you've been avoiding me."

Darn. "I haven't been avoiding you," he protested, even as an arrow of shame declared that wasn't true.

"Uh huh." She studied him with that level gaze all of the Reilly siblings possessed.

He really should've tried harder to pretend everything was okay. "What do you want me to see?"

"Come on."

He got his stuff, locked the door, then nodded to Jordan at the front cashier and asked him to lock up. Jordan agreed and Jasper followed Ellie out to the parking lot.

"You won't need your car," she said. "It's just a walk away."

He stored his stuff in his truck, then followed her, hands in his jacket pockets. He really hoped she wasn't about to introduce him to her boyfriend. Today had been tough enough that he didn't feel like he could cope with anymore.

She led him up the alley, past the site of the former hardware store which some enterprising locals had turned into a kind of indoor market called the Village Shoppes Emporium.

Then they were on Main, walking past Trinity Organics, and the tiny cinema that showed a lot of retro movies, to the lot that held the old museum. She turned into the path that led to the front door. Wait—the lights were on? She had a key? Was opening the door? What was going on? "Why do you have a key?"

She waved him inside the tiny foyer, and faced him with a smile. "Because you're looking at the new director of the Trinity Lakes Historical Museum."

"What?" Had his hints to Mrs. Darcy finally paid off?

"I know! I can hardly believe it either. My dream, handed to me on a platter. At least, it was." She frowned.

His heart stuttered. "What do you mean *was*?"

"It sounds so awful to say it out loud. But I know I can trust you."

"Sure," he said weakly. She could spill her dreams and he'd do all he could to see them come true. But if she had new dreams now...

"I'm excited, but also nervous, because I don't see this as something I'd do forever."

"You don't?"

She shook her head. "But that's okay. Olivia said it was just until reopening, then they'd revisit things again."

"What else would you do?" He'd thought this the perfect job for her, and maybe part of him had loved the fact it meant she'd be forced to stay, at least for a little while. But his main motivation for suggesting it had been knowing this was something she'd always longed to do.

"Travel. Study." Her glance shifted away and even in the dim light he could see her blush. "Jackson thinks I could marry one day."

His heart skipped several beats. Then sank like a rock in a pond when he realized she didn't mean him. Wait. Jackson didn't mean the French guy Cooper was talking about, did he? Things were that serious? They must be if all the family knew about it. Why hadn't he known?

He heaved out a shuddery breath and put his hands on his hips, pivoting as he pretended to check out the dusty building, when really, he couldn't stand her seeing his heart break. "Wow."

"I agree."

Oh no, she didn't. "When," he cleared his throat to sound less like a strangled cat, "when did you find out?"

"Last night. I think you heard Olivia Darcy ask me to dinner at church, right? She talked about it that night."

"So you're going to do it?"

She exhaled. "Well, that's what I wanted to ask you."

"Me?"

"Yeah. Mom and Jackson are all on board, but you know me well, too."

Not well enough, it seemed. She was thinking about marriage? He'd never dreamed—

"So, what do you think? I mean, I've prayed for God to direct my paths, but reopening the museum feels like such a huge thing." She moved into his line of sight again. "Do you think this is something I can do?"

Her blue eyes looked up at him, the vulnerability there kneading his selfishness into compassion. "You know I think you can do anything you put your mind to."

She beamed. "And that's why you're my best friend."

His heart wanted to cave in. He bolted a smile to his dial.

"So…" She dragged him to the dioramas. "I've been looking at all of this, and Olivia agrees, we really need a new exhibit that shows more than just what happened with the first white settlements. I mean, it's nice to have the history of the first settlers, but I just *know* the history of this whole land extends much further than when Lewis and Clark first explored the area back in 1806." She glanced up at him. "Don't you think?"

Truth be told it was hard to think, with her eyes shining up at him like that, her pink lips pursed into a smile. How could he have thought this was a good idea? Why had he ever thought he should put his own money into the role?

"What do you want me to do?"

"Well, I know it's a lot to ask, but I wondered if maybe Cohen's Hardware might like to sponsor us by providing the materials to do some renovation, and help create some new dioramas."

"Um…"

"It wouldn't be much, I promise," she said in a rush. "We're hoping we can get the whole town on board, including the school. Mrs. Kennedy has apparently got some students she thinks could earn extra credit by helping."

"Wow. Sounds like it's going full steam ahead."

"You know me. Once I have a project I like to get stuck into it."

He swallowed. "So, what does this mean about travel? Didn't you want to go back to Europe?"

"Yeah, well I still do. I promised Jackson I'd take care of the ranch stays—"

"That's happening now? I thought he was wanting to wait until summer."

"Yeah, well if I'd known this was going to happen then I probably wouldn't have said yes. But I didn't know so there's some people coming next week. And then, oh." Her cheeks pinked.

"Oh? What's oh?" His heart hammered.

"I haven't told you about Sebastian, have I? Not much anyway."

*Sebastian.* Already he hated him. "Who is he?"

"A guy I met in Paris. He's coming to visit me in the next week or two."

He pressed his lips together to stop the protest. Willed his expression to look casual, and not like she was shaking his world apart. "So a random guy from Paris is coming to see you?"

"Sebastian isn't random. He's very nice. We got along really well, and he wants to see me again."

"Yeah, well excuse me for being cynical, but how long have you known the dude for?"

Her eyes flashed. "That's none of your business."

He folded his arms to stop his heart from screaming and running away. "It is if you consider me a friend. I care about you, Ellie. And I don't love the idea of some guy you've barely known for five minutes coming to stay with you."

"He's not going to stay with me," she scoffed. "What do you take me for? He'll stay in the bunkhouse, like the other ranch stay guests."

The tightness in his chest eased partially. That was something at least.

"Why can't you be happy for me? I've been missing Europe, and it'll help to have a little bit of Europe come to Trinity Lakes."

"That's what souvenirs are for."

She rolled her eyes. "Honestly, you're acting like you're jealous."

"Of what?"

Her chin lifted, and she narrowed her gaze at him. He had no wish to be read by her so he looked away. "You're my friend, Ellie. I support you, but you know I'll always tell you what I think."

"Do you?"

"You know I do."

Her gaze held doubt, which was warranted. Because, yeah, there were some things he hadn't told her. But how could he admit the deepest longings of his heart? Especially now he knew she'd found someone who truly made her smile. "You know I'll do whatever I can to help you."

She exhaled. "I do know that. And that's why I asked you to come look." She pivoted on her booted heel. "Olivia said we can work around these other commitments, so I figured I've got just over seven weeks. If we work hard, we can get it done by Memorial Day."

"We?"

She drew close, her hand on his arm. His fingers clenched automatically, but she didn't seem to notice, her gaze fixed on him. "You just said you'd do whatever you could to help me, didn't you?"

He had. He winced internally. But if he stayed close and helped her then maybe she'd come to see him as more than just a friend. He nodded stiffly.

"Oh, thank you!"

She wrapped her arms around him and squeezed.

He exhaled. Just what had he got himself into?

CHAPTER FIVE

"Are you sure this isn't some delayed April Fools' prank?" Rhonda Ingalls frowned as she looked around the dusty, dated museum. "There is no way anyone can get this reopened by Memorial Day."

Ellie put her hands on her hips, willed her expression to look pleasant, and not like the gossipy busybody was voicing Ellie's own fears. "It certainly is true, and there certainly is a way." Ellie glanced at Jess's mom, Shona Martin, and Selena Palis from the Trinity Lakes Gazette, and the others who had responded to the social media invitation to join the museum reopening volunteers.

Jasper nodded, bolstering her spirits, enabling a more genuine smile for Rhonda. "As you can see by the number of people here, there are plenty of townsfolk eager to get things going again. Which means we need to be streamlined and intentional in our efforts, given the tight time frame. We'll need the support of as many people as possible, both with cleaning of the space and the current exhibits, preparing the museum reopening, and ongoing help with volunteers. Tonight's meeting is to see if those who are interested might

56

be able to volunteer some of their time for some of these things."

She held up a printout. "So I have a list of practical pre-opening day jobs, such as cleaning, carpentry, painting, visual or website design, photography, and research, so if you have skills in those areas, we'd love for you to put your name down to help. The other list," she held up a different piece of paper, "is for people who might be able to offer some time in an ongoing capacity either as a volunteer guide, or in finances or administration, and we'd like you to mark down how much time you can genuinely commit to. This will help us know what our opening hours will look like."

Ellie drew in a necessary breath. She might like to talk, but it felt like she hadn't talked this much in ages. And certainly not in front of so many people. "This is a community project, so the more volunteers the better, as we all know that many hands make the work a lot lighter." She smiled, willing it to deflect any negativity. "So, are there any questions?"

"Are any of the positions paid?"

Ah. Olivia Darcy hadn't prepped her for that particular question. "At the moment we need a commitment from people willing to volunteer their time. It may be revisited after we are generating an income from visitors." A glance at Olivia saw her nod.

"Are you telling me that you're doing all this for free?" Kyla Ferguson asked.

Olivia cleared her throat. "Naturally, the person responsible for spearheading such a thing deserves some degree of compensation."

"So that's a yes. And yet you're wanting everyone else to work for free. Hmph." She sat down with a scowl.

Ellie glanced at Olivia who rose to her feet.

"It may be of interest to some of you to learn an anonymous donation was made with the express purpose of paying someone to take on this role. The board felt that Miss Eloise Reilly was the best candidate for the position."

Another glance at Jasper showed his small smile. Her heart twinged in gladness. She was so thankful for his support.

"Now, if that is all concerning remuneration, perhaps we can continue with what else we might like the wonderful Trinity Lakes community to offer." Olivia waved a hand at Ellie. "Please continue."

"Thank you." Ellie swallowed. Forced a smile. "So, because this is a community initiative we were going to ask if anyone had any historical ledgers, letters, journals, or photographs, or any other items that you might like to donate for inclusion in the museum displays that help tell the story of Trinity Lakes. We already have a great range of items in the current displays, but there is room for more. I understand that some things may be precious and valuable to your family or not something that you wish to part with for insurance purposes. But if there are things that you feel would be helpful to demonstrate more of the community history then we would love for you to talk with us about that."

She took a breath. "Of course, some things would more naturally lend themselves to consideration for inclusion, like photographs, or old clothes or antiques. We ask that you search your attics and basements and those things in storage that just might prove of interest to a wider audience. And then, we'd need to consider what we already have and whether your item would be a duplicate or whether it provides something new. If it's the latter, then we'd love to see how we could go about including that as part of the town history display."

She smiled. "That concludes tonight's meeting. If you have any further questions, please talk with myself, Mrs. Darcy, Mrs. Kennedy or the other board members. And don't forget to please sign up with your availability to help both in the preparation for the museum reopening and whether you're able to assist with ongoing projects or exhibits. We would love to see as many people involved as possible."

Another glance at Jasper revealed his hand was partway up. "Oh, that's right. If you are at all handy then Jasper Cohen will be running a workday here this Saturday. We'll commence the construction of a few new dioramas as part of several new displays. What time are you meeting, Jasper?"

"From ten," he said. "And we'll be aiming to meet most Saturdays until opening day around Memorial Day Weekend."

She smiled gratefully at him, and he nodded, his arms folded, his own lips tweaking upwards for a moment before flatlining again. Something was still up with him. She didn't know what. She just knew she wanted to see him smile at her again like he used to. She hoped his own voluntary efforts weren't going to prove too great a strain. He obviously had a lot on his plate.

The room buzzed with conversation, and she was glad to see some names on the lists as she moved to the exhibits. When she'd first shown Jasper the museum, the temptation had been to get stuck in and clean it all herself. But he'd advised it was an opportunity for more community members to get invested and develop a sense of ownership for the museum. And hopefully seeing it at its dusty decayed worst would shock them into swift action.

Jasper was wise like that. Her tendency had always been to run ahead, but she could see the benefit in delay. So even though she kind of hated showing her vulnerable side—her need for others to contribute—she could see the value in having more people come on board to get things done.

"People want to feel valued and appreciated," Peter Franklin said later, when most of the others had left. "And asking them to help is a sure-fire way to get them passionate for the future."

Lexi nodded. "And there's something about cleaning that gives that instant lift, so it'll help with people feeling like their efforts are really making a difference."

So even though Ellie itched to get stuck in, she knew for the museum reopening to be sustainable they needed all hands on deck.

"How did you go finding volunteers to help?" she asked Jasper later.

"We'll have a crew." He shrugged. "It'll be good to shift some of those displays around. But you'll definitely be here?"

"With bells on."

His mouth twitched. "Can't wait to see that."

———

THURSDAY AND FRIDAY passed with ranch duties and more planning at night. She was exchanging emails and phone calls with Olivia Darcy and Marianne Kennedy and learning all kinds of interesting things. Like the role Marianne and her husband had played in adding some Australian flavor to Trinity Lakes, with everything from the Australian Football League games to the memorial service around April 25 for those who'd fought in the Australian and New Zealand Army Corp. She remembered Marianne teaching about Anzac day, how she used to bring Anzac biscuits—even though they were more like cookies—when she taught history at high school. So adding another exhibit devoted to that would be helpful.

She leaned back, studying the sketch she'd drawn of the museum's layout. Her nose wrinkled. Did they really need so much space devoted to the Wainscott family? How were they going to fit in the new native American exhibit? She sighed. Then called Jasper.

"You got a minute?"

"And hello to you too."

"Did I wake you?"

"It's nine at night, Ellie. I'm not that much of an old man."

"You sound grumpy."

He sighed. "Did you want something?"

"Can I come over?"

A beat passed. Two. "It's nine at night, Ellie. Can't this wait until tomorrow?"

"Oh. Okay. Sorry… we'll talk tomorrow then." She ended the call. Frowned at her phone. Why was Jasper so reluctant to talk to her?

Her phone flashed with an incoming call. She grinned. "Why good evening, Jasper."

"What did you want?"

"It's the museum layout. Can I send you a picture I've drawn?"

"I'm sure you can." His tone was dry.

"Okay, I'm taking a photo now," she snapped the pic, "and sending it your way. Let me know when you get it."

A ping alerted her even before he said, "It's here."

"Okay, see where the museum entry currently is? Do you think it'd get a bit squishy trying to move a lot of people through there? I know we have the geography exhibit, that leads to the agricultural display. I'm wondering if maybe we could add an extra couple of boards and display cabinets along the middle section there. Tabby Thomas indicated that they had a few antiques her family had inherited from their grandmother, some of which are said to date back to the Oregon Trail, so that could be fascinating to include."

"It's hard to know how that could work until we see the actual exhibits."

She sighed. "I should've asked for a deadline to donate, shouldn't I?"

"Hey, you're doing well. Especially when you've never done this before."

"Thanks." His soft words fueled courage. "I really thought it might be easier than this, especially as so many of the exhibits are already there. I don't know why I thought it would just be a simple dust and clean and reorganize. Sometimes this feels overwhelming."

"There's a reason Olivia Darcy thought you could do this," he encouraged. "I know you can, too."

"You're so sweet."

"Yep."

She smiled. "I don't know why you put up with me."

"An excellent question," he said. "Maybe it's because I've been doing this for so many years I don't know how else to be."

His words stroked comfort yet ignited pain. "Are we okay?"

He paused. "What do you mean?"

But even that small pause fueled uncertainty. "I feel like ever since I got home you've been a bit distant, a bit different around me. If I've done something to offend you, you just need to tell me. We're friends, Jasper. I'd hate to think that I've done something to upset you."

"I'm not upset." His voice sounded strained. "I am tired, though. Work is being extra fun, and it's tax season, so—"

"Oh, I should've realized. I'm so sorry. Is it too much for you, helping with the museum like this? You only need to say so. I'm sure Jackson or someone else can help run the workdays."

"I'm happy to help," he said firmly. "But if I seem distracted, it's just that there are a few things going on."

"Is there anything I can help with?" she asked.

"Says the woman who just admitted to feeling overwhelmed at times."

She laughed. "I mean it. I want to help you if I can. And if I've asked too much of you with the museum, then you only need to tell me. I don't want to put you under any extra pressure."

His chuckle sounded wry. "Yeah, thanks for the offer but I don't think you can help with this. It's something I need to figure out on my own."

"You don't have Albert Thomas to help you with the accounting side of things?"

He paused, ever so briefly. "Yeah, I do. Hey, I'll give it some thought. But I probably need to go now."

"Can we meet tomorrow night?" She could hear the reluctance as the seconds ticked away. "Hey, don't worry about it. I'll see you Saturday."

"It'll be okay, Ellie. You were born to do this."

"I sure don't feel that way sometimes. Some days I think I'd like to run away back to Paris."

"But that isn't really real, is it?" he said softly.

Indignation rose, followed by a swift clang of realization that he spoke the truth. For it wasn't enough to want to live elsewhere, to deny responsibility and hard work.

"You doing this is a good thing, an important thing for Trinity Lakes," he continued. "Like I said, you'll be fine."

Hmm. If he said so.

———

ELLIE MIGHT BE fine but he sure wasn't. Jasper glanced around the room where nearly a dozen volunteers were engaged in cleaning floors and windows, dusting off exhibits, and very carefully shifting display cases filled with treasure. Well, some might call it treasure but he struggled to understand the appeal of some of those things. Why would anyone want to keep an old apron? But for some reason Ellie thought it was essential and he wasn't going to argue with her about historical things. Even if he still burned to question why she thought she needed a French guy in her life. He thought his little comment the other day about Paris not being real would result in her being upset but she seemed to have taken it in her stride. All he could do was hope and pray that his little drops of common sense would help her see what was right.

For all he knew he might be wrong. Maybe this Sebastian dude was the man Ellie was supposed to be with, the one that God had arranged to be the biggest blessing in her life. But it didn't feel like it. Each day he was trying to commit his heart to God but as the days dragged nearer to Sebastian's arrival he felt the panic rise a little higher. Would she look at Sebastian and compare him to Jasper and see how far Jasper fell short? But honestly, how could she find someone she'd known for such a brief amount of time more appealing than a friend? Maybe it was his accent or the guy was Gilbert Blythe good looking. That was the standard by whom Ellie seemed to rate all men. He'd never forgotten the time she'd come over and watched an *Anne of Green Gables* movie with his mom and told Jasper he was a solid eight on the Gilbert scale of appeal. She'd said the only thing he needed to do to reach a ten was to start wearing waist-coats or boater hats, neither which held appeal. He was happy being an eight.

"The right gentleman will always appeal to the right lady," Mom had said.

Yeah, well, maybe that meant Jasper wasn't the right man for Ellie. Because she didn't seem to see him as holding any special qualities. Maybe he was too gentle. Or maybe he needed to develop an accent that made a girl swoon.

"Okay, that should just about do it. Oh! Mrs. Baxter, please be careful with the feathers in that bonnet. They need to be gently cleaned, not manhandled."

He glanced across to where Ellie was biting her bottom lip. One of the downsides of a public workday open to all volunteers was that some seemed to have as little idea as he did about just what made certain treasures treasured. He was glad his job consisted mostly of wielding a hammer and some wood and nails.

He finished leveling a shelf and used a level to check its evenness. Yep. Good.

"Hey boss," he called to Ellie. "Wanna come check?"

He didn't need her to check, but figured she needed a moment's respite. She'd been working hard when he arrived at nine this morning. Apparently she'd been here since eight. The floor had already been swept several times, but she didn't seem to mind that each movement of the cabinet released several decades worth of dust to the floor, thus requiring another sweep. Nobody could say she wasn't industrious.

"You know what I think we need?"

"What?" She looked like she needed a vacation.

"Some more of Marianne's Anzac cookies."

"Anzac biscuits," she corrected automatically.

He grinned. "You know that could be a fun bonus for visitors. An extra incentive for the first ten people each day: they get tea and coffee and an Anzac biscuit."

She sighed.

"What?"

"You keep coming up with good ideas and I just don't know that I have capacity to pull it all off."

"Who says you have to pull it all off? Nobody says this has to be the equivalent of the Guggenheim Museum on day one. We're a small-town museum. You don't have to have all of the internet stuff uploaded."

"But Mindy keeps telling me that that is the kind of thing that helps draw people's attention. It's all about SEO, whatever that stands for."

"Search Engine Optimization," he said.

"Why do you know that?"

He shrugged. "Because I've had to work on our marketing for the hardware store."

"You're full of surprises, aren't you?"

Oh yes, he was. "Anyway, you don't need to worry about that. That's the sort of thing you can do over time. I think your priority needs to be getting everything up to a standard that means opening day will be the success that you and Olivia and Marianne want. Which means preserving your energy to focus on those things that only you can really do. Anyone can clean, Ellie. But not everyone can make decisions about where things should be positioned. That's your domain."

"You're right. Again."

"Mister Right. That's me."

Her eyes widened, and he realized how that sounded. But couldn't think of any words that didn't sound lame so he turned away, pretending interest in a hammer. No way was he going to stand there and beg her to consider him. "I'm going to go get some more nails. Back in a sec."

He moved outside where a couple of students from the Bible College were doing some planting. A box hedge along the path and a few azaleas against the stonework of the museum's base should be grown and be in flower by the time summer rolled around. Provided this spell of milder weather continued, and they got some rain.

By the time he got his supplies and returned inside, the mood had dropped a little. Maybe the joy of cleaning had lost its zing. He nodded to Ellie. "You know, you could see if that phonograph still works."

Her eyes rounded. "You think we need mood music?"

"Either that or a round of curly fries and shakes from the diner."

"Of course! Motivation music and food. Wow, Jasper. You're so good at stuff like this, at managing people."

His lips tweaked. If only he was so good at managing his heart.

# CHAPTER SIX

"Welcome to Reilly Family Ranch." Ellie smiled and swept her arm to the path. "We're so glad you're here."

Marnie and her husband and their tiny tribe of two under-ten-year-olds grinned as they exited the vehicle. "Do you have horses?" Tommy, the little boy asked.

"Sure we do. What's a ranch without horses?"

"Can we go riding?" the girl asked.

"It's Becky, right?" She nodded. "Have you ridden before, Becky?"

"Only on a pony," she said.

"We have a pony here, brought in especially for you." From a nearby ranch that wanted to get rid of poor Mr. Ed.

"You didn't have to do that," Marnie said in an undertone.

Oh, but they did if they wanted to attract families to come and stay. "I think you'll find it a lot easier with two smaller horses for children to ride," Ellie said, with a smile.

"Good thinking."

"Now, if you'd like to come this way. Here, let me help you with your bags."

"I've got it," Marnie's husband said.

She took them on a new path, around the side of the house, which had recently received a quick repaint and refresh of the garden beds. God bless Cohen's Hardware and their special discount for family and friends. They neared the bunkhouse, to the section for their paying guests, newly screened off from the workers' accommodation. Marnie's family would be staying in the rooms where Jackson had stayed when Lexi was living here. He might've complained about missing Lexi when she returned to live with her folks in early November, but he also hadn't been shy about being glad to have the use of his bedroom again. The rooms here had ensuite bathrooms and while basic, she and Mom and Jackson had done their best to ensure that people would have some of the creature comforts of home.

"Where's the TV?" Tommy asked.

But not all. Ellie smiled. "You're on a ranch, honey. It's about the big open spaces and the animals and stars."

"That's right, sweetie." Marnie cast an anxious look at Ellie. "You don't need a TV. You can watch stuff at home, but you can't ride a horse so easily there."

"Or pat a pig. Or feed chickens. Have you collected eggs before?" Ellie asked, crouching to face Becky. "We have special chickens, they're really fluffy like a bunny."

"Bunny chickens?" Becky asked.

Ellie nodded. "They're actually called Chinese Silkies but we can call them bunny chickens if you prefer."

"I want to see the bunny chickens, Mommy." Becky's eyes were round.

"I'm happy to give you a tour if you like," Ellie said.

This was part of her role, Jackson had informed her. She would organize the bookings, and then do the welcomes and initial tour. Mom had agreed to do everything to do with food, from the welcome baskets (which included fruit, and homemade chocolate and cranberry muffins) to the breakfast baskets (which included an assortment of breads, pastries and cereals, milk, juice, yogurt and fruit), to be delivered each morning at a time specified by the guests. For the other main meals guests had to make their own arrangements. A handy binder listed several of the local options, including Joe's Diner, the Bellbird Café, the pizzeria, bakery and food truck options, as well as more distant restaurants in Walla Walla. But there was also a toaster, electric kettle, and coffee maker in each room, and it was hoped most guests would be happy enough to forgo a cooked breakfast and not create too much extra work for Mom and Ellie.

"I'll be outside near the horse trough when you're ready to see those chickens, okay?"

She exited the room, straightened the blanket on the rocking chair outside the door, and prayed that the Reilly version of welcoming would meet with their approval.

A short time later she was introducing an awed Becky and Tommy to the fluffy chickens, and after receiving Marnie's permission, sat the children down on a hay bale and placed the chicken on Becky's lap. "Now if you stroke her really gently, you'll see her cluck."

"Will she lay an egg on me?"

"I don't think so."

"Does she have a name?"

"No. Maybe you should think of a name for her?"

"Hmm. I like Henrietta."

"That's a great name," Ellie said. "Once you've finished giving Henrietta a gentle hug then I'll take you to meet the pig."

The next hour was spent taking them to see the various animals and sites: Doris the pig, Brutus the bull, the horses, cows, sheep, the fields where the solar farm glinted in the afternoon sun, and the distant view of the lakes that gave the town its name.

"It certainly is a slice of paradise," Marnie said.

"I've always thought so," Ellie agreed.

She paused. Seeing the ranch from another's eyes helped her realize just how lucky—how blessed—she was to live here. Sure, it wasn't Paris, but maybe Jasper had been right and that was a dream. A dream she'd been lucky enough to live in for a brief season, but one that she *had* lived. Just as others felt that staying in Trinity Lakes was like living in a dream. *Hey God, I'm sorry for being ungrateful.*

"And what else does Trinity Lakes offer?" Marnie's husband asked.

"Actually, we're about to reopen the historical museum, and there's a small cinema in town, and the Lakeside playground. We also have a few wineries nearby, and in summer there's a summer camp, and a little fun park, with minigolf, waterslides, and the like. And there's always boating, and kayaking."

"A thriving community, it seems."

"We do our best."

After checking they were happy to supervise the children using Ellie's childhood trampoline and swing set, she excused herself, her steps slow as she returned to the house. She *was* blessed to have grown up here. Imagine being a little kid stuck inside a city apartment, rarely getting the chance to run around and breathe fresh air, or do simple tasks like collecting eggs, things that she wanted for her own children, some day in the distant future. She wanted them to grow up in a thriving community, one that cared, where her kids could grow up with lifelong friends, as she had with Jasper.

And for the first time the thought of Sebastian's arrival next weekend didn't make her heart flutter one bit.

———

After the Sunday service, she saw the way Jasper wore weariness. It had been enough to prompt her to invite him to lunch at Joe's Diner, before his hesitation made her question her impulsiveness again.

"We always go there," he said, tilting his head at Jackson, who was engrossed in conversation with Lexi and her folks.

"Oh. Right."

His smile was bleak. "Sorry. I'm just not in the mood for another inquisition from your brothers."

"What do you mean?"

"Nothing." He glanced away.

"That doesn't sound like nothing. What have they said to you?"

He shrugged. "Every time they see me and you together they ask awkward questions about my intentions."

"Your intentions—? Oh. Wow. That's ridiculous." Wasn't it? She studied him closely. "Is that why you've been a little distant in recent weeks."

"I don't think you can accuse me of being distant when we've been working alongside each other the past two Saturdays, and you call me nearly every night."

She winced. "When you put it like that, I sound kind of annoying."

"You've been busy. I get it. How did things go with your first ranch stay guests?"

"Awesome. I wondered at first if the kids would cope with a TV detox but they seemed to still have fun. Mom and I found a whole bunch of board games and I think they now have a new appreciation for Twister." She grinned. "Remember when we used to play that?"

He nodded.

"Anyway, it went well, and I'm pretty sure Marnie wants to book again in the summer. So it was nice to prove to Jackson that it was okay to do this earlier than he'd intended."

"Imagine that, Ellie wanting to prove her big brother wrong."

"I know, right?" She grinned. "I've never had anything to prove."

"Unlike some of us."

"Yes, you with the interrogations. You poor thing."

His laughter sounded forced. "Hey, if they're like that with me, I'd love to see what happens when your Paris friend gets here."

Oh. Sebastian. Right. So far her brothers and mom had been a little surprised about the proposed arrival of Ellie's French man-friend, but they'd barely said anything, like they thought Sebastian a figment of an over-romantic imagination. Clearly Jasper didn't think of him in such terms. She studied him, as a muscle throbbed in his jaw.

His gaze swung to hers again. "When does he arrive again?"

"Saturday."

He nodded. "So you won't be at the museum."

She winced again. "It sounds bad when you put it like that, huh?"

He gave a small shrug. "Only if you care what the likes of Rhonda Ingalls and Kyla Ferguson think."

"You know," her voice dropped to a whisper, "I don't really think I do."

His smile flashed, a real, genuine smile, and it warmed her heart so much she grinned back, looping her arm through his. "That's the smile I love to see. And now you've pointed out my flaws, are you prepared to suffer the barrage of opinion and let me buy you lunch as a thank you for all your hard work?"

He exhaled heavily. "If you insist."

"I do."

His lips flattened. "Then let's go."

———

"Okay, now I need you to hold it here."

It was Sunday afternoon, and while normally Jasper would consider it a day of rest, he'd found himself—once again—unable to say no when Ellie had begged for his help with cutting boards for a new diorama while he'd been enjoying his Trinity burger and shake.

"Marianne has said some of the kids at school are going to illustrate it—they've got these special computer graphics they're using that can be glued on—but I need to get them to her asap. And I feel so bad knowing I won't be able to help much next Saturday, so if you can show me what I can help with now that'd be awesome."

And take up what previous free time he had in the week? "I'd planned to watch a hockey game."

"Oh." Her nose wrinkled. "I forgot. Mitchell only has a few more games left in the season, so I should probably be a good sister and watch that too."

He knew this was a bad idea. Spending time with her always fueled the hope for more. But his mouth hadn't caught the memo. "We could watch it together after."

"After you help me?"

"I thought you were supposed to be helping me," he countered.

"Well, I think we both know that you're the expert, although I might be the more enthusiastic one of us both."

"That you are for sure." One of the things he loved about her. Her ability to take life by the horns and keep astride even when life bucked and kicked and threatened to dump her over and over again. First with growing up without a dad. Then forced to work at the ranch. Then missing out on college. She'd never complained. He'd always been impressed by her willingness to keep riding, one arm in the air as she whooped and hollered and laughed and smiled. He always thought things through so many times that second guessing might as well be his middle name. Like, he'd probably still be mulling over whether reopening the museum was a good idea, yet she'd jumped in, boots and all. But her zest contrasting with his caution was part of why they made a good pair.

A stubborn thought persisted that they *would* make a good pair. And that this might be the last time to prove that to her before her French dude showed up and got her questioning things again.

"Okay then. Let's do it."

He drove her to the hardware store where he collected supplies that he paid for himself, then drove her to his house. After greeting his mom—Dad was having a rest after the service this morning—they collected the materials and moved to the workshop out the back.

His dad's neat-freakness had passed down to him, and he looked around with pride, smiling a little as Ellie sighed.

"I don't think any room in our house has ever looked as tidy as your workshop."

"It's what Cohen men do." And meant life was a heck of a lot easier. Why wouldn't you hang a tool in the correct spot so you'd save time looking for it? "Okay, have you got the measurements?"

She slapped her backside. "Right here." Then drew out a piece of paper from her jeans pocket and handed it to him.

He glanced at the figures, trying to ignore the way she hovered close, the scent of her hair—the fragrance of her—drifting to take his senses prisoner. How could she not have any idea of her effect on him? He slowly exhaled, and moved to the bench where the jigsaw sat ready and waiting.

Five minutes later, earmuffs on, the saw was ripping through the wood to the dimensions she'd given him. She wanted a curved backdrop for the new Native American exhibit that the students would paint, which required mountains and canyons and the river gorge. The exhibit would have extra depth and dimension, and once painted would really draw the eye.

She tapped his shoulder. He switched off the saw and removed his earmuffs. "Can I try?" She grinned. "I don't mind watching a muscly man do his thing but I'm not exactly helping."

He resisted the urge to flex. "You've used a saw like this before, right?"

"A million years ago, back when we made props for the school musical."

He nodded. They'd worked together, and he'd taught her what he'd known. "It's been a few years, then. Here's a quick refresher."

Okay, so he wasn't above shifting close so he could hold her hands for the best position. Her breath might've hitched—his sure did—but he pushed past it, explaining about the 'shoe' and the blade and the upstroke.

She nodded, her ponytail tickling his nose. "I got this."

"Okay." He released her and stepped back. "Let's see how you go."

The next half hour passed with his instructions, her sawing, his nods of approval as she followed the lines marked on the boards until he was confident she could do it.

He moved to the other workshop table, and using the miter saw began a series of crosscuts to enable the frames to stand. If he got this done now then it could get sanded and painted next weekend. By someone else while she picked up her French guy.

His heart stuttered. But he'd make the most of his time with her now. Revel in her smiles. In her appreciation. In her tease.

Their banter continued over the next hour until she'd finally finished the last cut, and he angled in the last cut to prep the frame so it could stand.

"Wow. I can't believe we've done so much," she said, hands on hips.

"You've done well. I reckon we could make a carpenter out of you yet."

She made a face at that, then placed her arms around his torso. "Thank you so much, Jasper." She squeezed him. "You're the best."

He wrapped his arms around her, pressed his lips to her forehead, and closed his eyes. Then lingered, as time seemed to slow, the busyness of recent hours, days, weeks fading until there was nothing but him and her. Her. And him. Together. Alone. Nobody else intruding. Private. Quiet. Sacred. And his opportunity to finally show her what he'd been feeling. He smiled. Given Jasper and Ellie's connection, the French dude never had a chance.

Her arms tightened around his middle. His heartbeat rocketed. Was that her invitation? Would she welcome his embrace?

Then she murmured, "Jasper?"

Her head tilted, and his lips skimmed down her nose.

"What are you do—?"

His lips found hers, swallowing the last of her question as he finally dared to do what he'd dreamed of for so long. Her lips were so soft, so sweet, he could taste the strawberries that decorated the top of her milkshake before. Fire arced between them and he shifted to hold her more closely, one hand around her waist, the other tracing the softness of her cheek. Then realized any passionate response was one-sided, as she'd frozen, was still and stiff in his arms, her lips unmoving under his. He opened his eyes, peeked at her. She stared at him wide-eyed. *Dear God, no.*

He released her, and she instantly stepped away, as if she couldn't stand to be closer to him than six feet away. His heart crumpled, then broke some more as her expression morphed into confusion, edged with something he really hoped wasn't horror.

She touched her lips. "What... what was that?"

Um, the best moment of his life? Until it turned into quite possibly the worst.

"You kissed me." So she'd noticed. "You *kissed* me, Jasper. Why?"

Anything he said now would either tip this friendship into truth and possibly break it forever, or he could somehow salvage things with a small fib.

Still, a man had to speak the truth, even if right now he felt like a man armed only with a butter knife attempting to chop down a fierce jungle to find the city of gold. But only those who dared to venture ever won, right? He swallowed. *Please Lord, let me win.* "You know I like you, Ellie. You know I've always cared—"

"But not like that. We're friends. We're *only* friends, Jasper."

She didn't mean that, surely. But that look on her face suggested she did. Any hope she might be open to more shriveled up and died. Stuff the truth. He needed to save this situation, save his pride, otherwise they wouldn't even be friends.

"Which is why," he continued, *God, forgive him,* "I thought you needed practice."

Her eyes rounded. "Practice?"

He shrugged, shoved his hands in his back pockets. "For when your friend from Paris comes. He's French, and they're all about romance, right? So he's not coming all this way not to French kiss you."

Her mouth fell open, her cheeks blazing to bright pink. "I'm not going to French kiss him."

He suddenly had the weirdest feeling they weren't talking about the same thing. Then he blinked as he realized what he'd said. "Whoa. I did not mean *that.*"

"Are you out of your mind?"

Quite possibly.

She scowled. "And what's with needing your help? Did you honestly think I've never kissed a guy before?"

She had? "Who?"

Her fists flew to her hips. "I'm not about to kiss and tell."

She'd kissed someone else? How had he not known? Who'd dared touch perfection? How could she not want him? Rejection slashed, an angry dragon that had gouged his soul. He needed her to leave so he could curl up in a whimpering ball. He had to settle instead for hands raised in surrender, and a mask of nonchalance like she hadn't thrust a stake through his heart. "My mistake. Sorry. It won't happen again." Not until the proverbial froze over.

A noise stole their attention to the door. His dad stood there, glancing between them, worry in his brow. "Hey, is everything okay out here?"

No. He was finding it hard to breathe. His heart was bleeding out. "Sure."

Ellie rubbed at her mouth, as if trying to remove every last molecule of Jasper's DNA from her lips. "We're fine."

Jasper's gaze flew to hers. Were they? Had their friendship survived his ill-fated attempt at romance? She looked away.

"Ellie. It's good to see you."

"You too, Mr. Cohen. You're looking well."

"Ah, it helps to have someone helping out more at the hardware, helping you out too, I see."

Ellie nodded, her smile artificial.

"I've got a good son here." He clapped Jasper on the shoulder.

A good son who'd just assaulted a woman with his lips. He rubbed a hand over his jaw. "Was there something you wanted, Dad?"

"Just to tell you the game's about to start." He nodded to Ellie, as Jasper's mom joined them too. Great. "I thought someone might like to join us to see her famous brother do his thing."

"Oh, thank you Mr. Cohen, but—"

"Aww, don't go giving us an excuse," his mom said. "It's been ages since you watched some hockey with us, when you used to do so all the time. I've made honey soy chicken wings. That used to be your favorite, right?"

Bless his parents for trying to help but, "Mom, I really think —"

"It sure would be fun to watch it again with someone who might know a thing or two about what's really going on behind the scenes."

Dad wouldn't be saying that if he knew what had just gone down behind the scenes here. And no way did Jasper want to sit next to Ellie and pretend everything was still the same. Because it wasn't. Jasper had broken it. He'd broken *them*. And nothing could ever be the same again. His heart caved in a little more. What had he done?

"Please, Ellie?"

Apparently Jasper would need to give his parents a good talking-to as soon as Ellie left.

"Ah, sure, Mr. Cohen." Ellie's gaze shifted to Jasper, instantly morphing to steel. *No funny business*, her laser glare screamed.

Yeah, that sure wouldn't be a problem. She'd made her point crystal clear. No way was he ever going to step from the friend zone again.

That was, if she even still considered them to be friends.

# CHAPTER SEVEN

All through the game she'd kept herself still, sure any move would break the illusion. Part of her was in denial of what had just happened. Jasper's actions had rocked her to her core, tipping her world on its axis, like everything she thought she knew had been turned upside down. Just what had he done? Sure, she knew it was a kiss, but the gnawing question of *why* wouldn't leave her alone. She wasn't buying his 'she needed practice' story. His lie, really. For she'd seen that look of desperate hope in his eyes before her words had snuffed it out.

And it was the fact he'd lied to her that had shifted things almost as much as his kiss had. For how could best friends ever trust each other when someone lied? And now, she didn't know what to do, except she felt trapped in the Cohen's living room. But no way was she going to deny poor Mr. Cohen something he obviously wanted, like watching her brother score a goal, while she wondered who else had been so lucky to score his son's kiss.

Jasper's kiss.

She shivered.

"Are you cold, dear?" Mrs. Cohen asked. "There's a woolen

throw at the end you can use. The nights are still a little cool, aren't they?"

"Thanks. Yes, they are."

Ellie obeyed the implied request—after the scene in the Cohen's workshop before she had zero desire to cause anymore fuss—and snuggled deep into the folds scented with lavender. She peeked across. Jasper sat at the other end of the sofa, his posture as stiff as when he'd first sat down. He'd barely moved a muscle.

She didn't blame him. After scoffing a few spicy-sweet wings which had required a chaser of lemonade, she'd barely moved either. She didn't know what to do. What to say. She couldn't even look at him without feeling the terrible heavy weight of awkwardness blanketing everything.

Jasper liked her. As more than friends. And it was such a shock she didn't know what to do with that.

She stole another peek across at him. Met instead with Mr. Cohen's grin which tugged out her own. Fake smile. Fake friendship. She really should leave—

"How about that goal, huh? Mitchell's done okay this season, hasn't he?"

She nodded. More fake smiles. She really didn't care about her brother's hockey exploits. Right now, Mitch seemed as distant from reality as her supposed friendship with Jasper had proved to be. She really needed to leave. But Jasper's parents had always been so kind to her. They'd been the parents she'd gone to when her own hadn't been around, her father by choice, her mom by the demands of ranch life. But even leaving was problematic. She'd come in Jasper's truck. She could walk back to church, but it was several miles. Maybe she could message Jackson. He might still be at Lexi's place...

She tugged out her phone. Tapped out a message.

Jasper glanced at her. Glanced away. She could tell he was

itching to know what she was doing, but she wasn't going to tell.

Her phone flashed. Jackson: *Sorry, back home already.*

Darn.

Jasper's eyes were on her again. He lifted a brow. She glanced away. Maybe it was childish, but she didn't know how to talk to him, how to deal with someone she'd considered a friend who'd proved to have a very different understanding of the word. How long had he felt this way? Maybe that explained the too-long hug at the airport. Those too-long glances. Her chest grew tight. And stupid her had never realized…

"Want me to take you back?"

She pressed her lips together. Managed a nod. Managed a smile she hoped looked gracious for his parents. "Thank you so much for dinner."

"Nice to watch a game with you again," Mr. Cohen said, shifting in his chair.

"No, don't get up." She rubbed his shoulder, and accepted a hug from Mrs. Cohen who studied her as they moved to the hall slowly following Jasper outside.

"You two were so quiet," Mrs. Cohen said. "I've never heard you say so little to each other before. Is everything okay between you?"

Ellie nodded. It would be. Once she was by herself and had the luxury to think. And once he'd apologized. How dare he treat her like that? How could a friend treat her that way?

She blinked back tears and turned, stifling an inclination to ignore him and go walk through the dark to her car anyway.

She opened the passenger door and got in, eyes straight ahead as she slumped as close to the door as possible without slipping out.

He seemed to notice, sighing, before he started the vehicle and eased down the drive.

The tension seemed to build the closer they got to the

church. A persistent thunder within demanded to know when he'd properly apologize, when he'd explain. She deserved an explanation. But it was something he should offer. It wouldn't mean as much if she demanded it.

Her fingers curled into fists as he turned into Main. He slowed as he drew close to the church where her car waited forlornly, the one vehicle in the dim parking lot.

She opened her door.

"I'm sorry," he muttered.

She shook her head. "I don't… I can't… I don't even know what to say."

When he didn't say anything more she finally found courage to sneak a peek at him. He was rubbing his jaw, his other hand holding the steering wheel in a white-knuckled grip, his expression blank as he stared out the windshield.

This was supposed to be when he explained himself, when he offered more than a pathetic two words of apology. Surely she—their friendship—deserved more? "Is that really all you've got to say?"

His lips pressed together, his Adam's apple dipping as a muscle ticked in his shadowed jaw. But he said not a word. Nothing. Nada. Done.

Anger rose fueled by fresh frustration. How could he sit there like he was unaware that everything had changed? Did he not realize what he'd done? Was he really so clueless that he didn't know he'd wrecked everything? Angry words formed, spilled.

"You've wrecked everything you know."

He finally turned to face her, his eyes glistening in the dark. "I know."

She slammed the door, and strode to her car, conscious he was watching, waiting to make sure she was okay. Like she could ever be okay again.

And it was only much, much later, when she'd huddled on

her bed, having sobbed and raged and relived every second of the highs and lows of the strangest afternoon of her life, that she wondered if that glisten had been tears.

———

"Hey there, sleepyhead."

Ellie scowled at her brother in the pre-dawn light and moved to the coffeemaker. Forget feeling like an English countess. After the worst sleep of her life she needed coffee. Stat.

"Whew. You had that much fun at Jasper's, huh?"

"Shut up."

"What? You expect a man not to notice when his sister begs for a car ride, then comes home looking like she's singlehandedly ready to take on the next zombie apocalypse?"

Her fingers gripped the mug handle as she waited for the trickle of brown gold to reach a satisfactory level. Breathe in through her nose, out through her mouth. Count to ten, and all that.

"Do I need to speak to him?"

"Nope."

"Then how about you fill me in?"

"How about you butt out of my business?"

Jackson's eyebrow rose. "Like that, is it? Something did go down."

She snatched the mug, but her movement was so fast she splattered some coffee on her sweater. "Great. Look what you made me do."

"Yeah, that's on you, sis. Literally."

She left before she was tempted to hurl the mug at him. Well, she was *tempted*, but before she actually followed through.

She had to get herself under control. Had to pretend all was right with the world. She had no desire for her nosy brother to go asking Jasper tricky questions. Although, it would be interesting to know what he'd say when facing her brother's grilling.

She changed her top, put her coffee-decorated sweater in the washing machine, and exited through the back door so she wouldn't have to speak to Jackson again.

An hour later, having completed her early morning chores, she was freed for breakfast, which thankfully Jackson wasn't present for. She poured her granola, topped it with milk, straight from Daisy the cow. Marnie and her kids had loved the fact they had fresh milk, even if it tasted different from what they were used to. She joined her mother at the table.

Her mom looked up at her from where she was mending a hole in one of Jackson's t-shirts. "I didn't expect to see you up so early."

"Thank the body clock that only knows to sleep in when I've gotten back after a day on a plane."

Her mother smiled. "You seem more settled now. Do you feel that way?"

She shrugged. She had been starting to. Her stomach tensed. Until last night.

"I thought I'd give the windows a clean today, seeing it's going to be nice weather. It's good to make the most of it and get things looking nice for when your friend comes to visit. Are you free to help me with the outside windows later?"

"Sure." She appreciated her mother's efforts. She should try a little harder too. Not that Sebastian would mind. Sebastian. She really needed to get her thoughts on him and not the traitor friend.

"So, I was thinking, maybe it is a little ungracious for you to have a visitor come from halfway across the world and put him in the bunkhouse. How would you feel if we had him stay in Mitchell's old bedroom instead?"

"Oh. I, uh," didn't care right now where Sebastian stayed. All she could think about was Jasper and his kiss. "Sure."

"I'm sure Jackson won't mind."

Yeah, she wasn't so sure about that judging from his earlier comments, and the way he'd insisted on sleeping in the bunkhouse when Lexi had stayed last year to help nurse Mom. But hey, if Mom said it was okay, nobody could complain, could they?

"Have you got much to do at the museum this week, Ellie?"

"A bit." A lot. Try, too much. She needed to check on the donations. Organize rosters. Set up a consult with the local elders regarding the Native American display. Finalize the wording for the website. Oh. And somehow get those freshly cut boards from the Cohen's house to the high school so they could be painted and prepped.

The thought of having to go to the Cohen's—to potentially see Jasper—suddenly seemed so huge, that stupid tears appeared again.

"Honey?" Her mother wrapped her in a hug. "It's okay. You'll manage."

"Mm hm." She breathed in her mom's scent of violets and soap.

"It'll be nice for you to spend some time with your friend. I've planned a special dinner for Saturday night. Did you want to invite some friends or just keep him to yourself?"

Friends? She stiffened. She knew who wouldn't say yes to that invitation any time soon. "I'm too tired to think. When do you need to know by?"

"Later in the week is fine." Her mom rubbed her back.

"Thanks Mom." Ellie gave her mom a gentle squeeze, her gaze dropping to the pile of clothes to be darned and mended.

"And I don't know what's happened between you and Jasper, but that'll work out too. You'll see."

"How do you know?"

"You've been friends for years. And every time you've argued you've always worked things out between you."

She hugged her mom closer. Except this time, it felt like a rip in their friendship that could never be repaired.

———

"THERE YOU GO, MRS. KENNEDY." Jasper propped the boards in the history teacher's room. "All prepped and ready for action."

"Oh, that's wonderful. I wasn't expecting it quite so soon. Ellie told me that she would need to arrange for it to be dropped off later in the week. I didn't realize she'd spoken to you already."

He forced a smile. She hadn't. He wondered if she'd ever talk to him again. But after the horror of Sunday afternoon, he'd avoided explanations with his parents about the obvious strain with Ellie and said he'd needed to finish the boards, as he tilted between exhilaration and frustration at what he'd done. But really, there was little to be excited about. He'd gone and misread her and messed things up completely. And now she was furious with him, ignoring his apology, his texts left unanswered like she'd blocked him. He wondered if she wanted to block him from her life.

But that was one of the curses of small-town life. People's lives intertwined with each other, and sooner or later he knew he'd see her. He'd be forced to talk to her in front of others where they'd need to pretend everything was normal. When really, they both knew his actions meant normal was no longer possible.

After waving off Marianne's thanks he made his way back to the hardware store. Ellie's visit seemed to have added pep to his father's spirits, and he'd determined to come to the store for a few hours each day this week. Which was good. Dad could wrestle with the finances while Jasper worked off his frustrations out the back, muscling equipment, hardware and building materials, the heavier the better. He'd love to get so exhausted he could drop into bed and sleep. And not dream.

"Hey, Jasper."

He nodded to Mr. Martin, and went through the Employees Only door to the section out the back that served tradesmen.

He was partway through shifting a concrete birdbath when his phone rang. He ignored it, lugging the ugly monster to the yard where the plants, garden ornaments and supplies were stocked. He carefully hauled it down, repositioning it slightly so it didn't scare customers of good taste. It was a special order for Mrs. Gilbertson, but she hadn't paid the first installment by the due date, so now, as per store policy, it was available for anyone to buy.

"That is one ugly sight."

His gaze lifted. Jackson. But he was looking at the birdbath, not him. Tense heartstrings eased. "Hey."

Jackson nodded. "Got a sec?"

Nope. Especially not with Ellie's brother. Was he here to read the riot act? "I'm pretty busy," he hedged.

"I get it. Just thought I'd call in on the off chance you needed a burger."

"It's not even twelve."

"Doesn't stop the need for a good feed. But hey, I'll catch you later."

"'Kay."

Weird. Jackson actually walked away. Then pivoted back around. "Did you say something to upset Ellie?"

"What? No." He hadn't said something. He'd done something, though. Then his ears caught Jackson's second-to-last word. "Is she upset?"

"I can't tell if it's because of something that happened on Sunday night or if she's just stressed about this coming Saturday."

"What's happening this—? Oh."

Jackson's face twisted. "Yeah, I can't say that I'm that excited about having some French guy come and stay in our house either but it is what it is."

"He's staying in your house? I thought she said he was staying in the bunkhouse."

Jackson made that face again. "Yeah, I thought that too, but apparently Mom thinks it'll be more welcoming for a European dude to feel at home in a home, if you know what I mean."

Jasper's chin dipped, as he fought the protest begging to escape his clenched jaw.

"I can't say that I'm pleased about it," Jackson confessed. "It's a good thing I've got to take Brutus on a tour of some of the local ladies soon."

"Wait—you mean you won't be there when he's staying in the house?"

"Yeah, but Mom will be. And I'll only be away for a few nights."

Jasper shook his head and glanced away.

"My sister can take care of herself," Jackson said softly. "My mom can too."

His gaze swung back to meet Jackson's. "At least tell me you'll be here for a few days when he arrives so you can see if he checks out."

"You don't trust him?"

"How can anyone? The guy met her two months ago and is already flying around the world to see her again? What kind of guy does that?"

"The kind who might be in love."

Jackson's words slapped him, reminding him of the guy who'd wanted to travel to England but had been stopped by circumstances. Not that it would've made any difference, apparently. Not when she'd made up her mind that the man she wanted—the man she'd prefer to kiss—was French. The guy must love her to come all this way. Did that mean she loved him too? "They hardly even know each other," he muttered.

"But he will, if he's around. Come on. He makes her happy."

This conversation was making him unhappy. "I need to go."

"Sure. Hey, we on for another game this Thursday?"

And have to dodge twenty questions with Ellie's brother? "Sorry. I'm booked." He would be, once he figured out what else he'd be doing.

"Okay. Oh, Mom wondered if you were free Saturday night."

"Why?"

"Apparently she wants to do a welcome to America dinner for Sebastian." Jackson rolled his eyes. "Lexi has agreed, and Coop is coming up."

"Sounds like it's just family." And that he wouldn't be welcome.

"And you're like family, dude." Jackson punched his arm. "I'm surprised Ellie hasn't mentioned it."

Jasper wasn't. Not one bit. The only surprise was that she hadn't warned him to stay away.

"I'll tell Mom you're a yes."

"What? No. I'm pretty sure I've got something going on."

"Yeah, I'm pretty sure you don't. Come on. Aren't you the least bit curious about the dude?"

Curious? A bit. Jealous? The whole nine yards.

"This'll be your chance to check him out and make sure he's suitable for our Ellie."

*Our* Ellie? His heart roared. Ellie wasn't his. She'd made it clear she had no wish to be. And he really didn't want to be inserting himself in a situation where it would quickly become evident that he was only there out of jealousy. Besides, she'd see right through him.

"I really don't think this is a good idea," he said firmly.

"Yeah, the more I think about it, the more I think it is good.

Who knows her better than you and me? So who better to give the big, bad brother warning than us?"

"Except I'm not her brother," he said stiffly.

Jackson studied him, his eyes widening slightly. "Dude. No."

At the look of pity in his eyes, Jasper's heart pinched. Nope. This was not helpful and definitely not how he wanted to spend his day. "Sorry man. I got work. Catch you later."

"Jasper, wait."

But he couldn't. He could never admit to Ellie's brother how he'd failed. How he'd selfishly tried to push for more when she didn't want anything to do with him. Jackson would likely punch him a lot harder—and in the face, not the arm.

So he brushed past him, digging out his phone as he pretended to get a call, until he went through the employee's door again and found a dark unused office where he could hide and lick his wounds in private. He closed his eyes. *God, help me.*

# CHAPTER EIGHT

Ellie bounced on her toes, excitement rippling through her. In a matter of minutes now—she could count the seconds—Sebastian would be here and all would be right with the world. Around her, the slow busyness of the airport continued, with conversations, reunions, farewells. She stood, waiting pretty near the exact same spot Jasper had waited for her nearly a month ago.

Her fingers clenched, then released. In some ways she almost resented the way that Jasper had stolen her anticipation of today by his actions last weekend. She'd spent far too much time replaying his hug, his kiss—his *kiss*—instead of having time to contemplate the dream-become-real that was Sebastian. Thanks to Jasper, her thoughts had been soured, edged with doom, instead.

But no. Today was not a day to think on such things. Today only Sebastian would fill her thoughts. Would he be as excited to see her as she was him? Would he hug her? More?

An excited shiver rippled up her spine. Sebastian was handsome, with a kind of European flair that lent itself to elegant clothes, cheekbones and floppy hair. She couldn't see him in holey t-shirts and dirt-stained jeans. Misgiving creased her chest. Would he fit in? She'd been amazed that he'd been interested in her, even more amazed when the communication kept going. And now he was here?

Truth be told she'd thought he'd like someone like Lexi. Lexi, whose cool Audrey Hepburn vibe had her wearing scarves and heels and silk and make-up that Ellie had never really known how to wear. She'd always felt stuff like that wore her instead. But maybe he saw the diamond past the rough. Like Jasper seemed to.

No! She wasn't thinking about him. She was thinking about —

"Sebastian!" She grinned and waved, and his face lit up.

*"Ma cheri."*

She hurried forward and he placed his bag on the ground, waiting with a smile as she moved to him. "Welcome to America! I can't believe you're here."

"It's so good to see you."

He hugged her and she leant against his wiry strength, drawing in the wonder of his being here, as his hands slid to her neck. Then he pulled back and clasped her face in his hands, and she closed her eyes as he kissed one cheek then the next, then with a soft sigh his mouth found hers.

Oh! Her eyes flew open. That was unexpected.

She pulled away, wishing she had taken another breath mint. Who knew what her breath smelled like? Hopefully he hadn't been able to taste anything over the coffee he'd obviously recently had. "Um, are you ready?"

His eyes sparked, and his mouth ticked up on one side. "Certainly."

"Did you have another bag?"

*"Oui."*

"Come on. This way."

She tugged him to the baggage claim, and when he pointed

to his bag she hefted it off the conveyor belt. "Did you pack rocks in here?" she joked.

"*Non.* Just a few gifts for your mama, and for you."

The intensity in his eyes made her shiver. Oh, this was what romance felt like. With none of that awful awkwardness she'd felt with Jasp—

"So, have you figured out how long you can stay?" she rushed to say. Maybe if she talked fast and loud she'd drown out the stupid voices in her head. "We're really flexible, you'll be staying in my brother's room—"

"Your brother?" He frowned. "I thought I'd be in my own room."

"Oh no. Mitchell is away. He lives in Minnesota so you're safe. We do have my other two brothers staying with us at the moment, Jackson and Cooper, although both of them have got work and will be away a bit in the next few weeks."

"So I'll have you to myself?"

"My mom is still there."

He nodded and followed her to her car. He smiled. "This is much smaller than I imagined a cowgirl needing."

She chuckled. "I'm not really a cowgirl, and to be honest, I've never been too fond of those vehicles with horns decorating the front."

He laughed. "Like in *The Dukes of Hazzard.*"

"*Exactement.*"

"*Tres bien.*"

See? Her Duolingo practice was working. Jasper had always thought she was a bit obsessed, but she'd proved him wrong—no!

"So, you want to try some American fast food before we go? It'll be over an hour until we're home, but I know that Mom has planned a special meal tonight."

"That'd be good. Airplane food is terrible."

She steered to the nearby street lined with fast food outlets, then paid for his fully loaded cheeseburger meal and shake. He'd need to change his money, but when she'd asked if he wanted to do it at the airport he'd insisted he just wanted to get home to see her place and he could change it at a bank at Trinity Lakes. She wasn't sure whether euros could be easily exchanged at First National but he had a credit card he could use, no doubt. Anyway, he was here. With her. She felt like the heroine in a romcom, grinning from ear to ear as he held her hand—when he wasn't eating—and they talked and laughed on the way home.

His exclamations of delight turned to comments about the landscape. "Have you had a drought?"

"Sometimes we do, but this winter has been wet."

He nodded, brightening when they approached Walla Walla. "It seems busy."

"It's a college town, so there are lots of businesses to support that. There's a prison nearby too."

His eyebrows rose but he said nothing more. She pointed out some landmarks: the golf course, the tiny airport, then the farms and ranches as they neared Trinity Lakes.

"So tell me about your home town again."

There was something special about having an extremely attractive man giving her his undivided attention. Something that really made her want to focus on him and not the road. But there'd be time for that, soon enough. So she told him about Trinity Lakes, about its natural beauty, its close-knit population, its quaint main street and quirky Australian connection. "I told you about the museum I'm reopening?"

He shook his head.

Huh. She was sure she'd mentioned something. Oh well. She told him about that, and reminded him that she'd need to devote some of her time to making sure things were progressing as they ought.

"You could come with me, explore the town, meet some of my friends."

"*Oui.*"

"Or if you don't want to you can always hang around at the ranch. There's always plenty to do there." She peeked at him. "Do you ride?"

"Horses?"

She nodded.

"*Non.*"

"Ah, well, I can teach you. Or Jackson can, or Denny."

"Who is this Denny?" He frowned. "Is he a boyfriend?"

"Denny?" She laughed. "He's the ranch foreman, and about sixty give or take a day. You don't need to worry about him. Or anyone else."

Conviction panged. For all she'd told Jasper about her previous kissing experience, she could now count her kisses on two fingers. Three, if you counted the boy who'd kissed her on a dare when they were six. She pushed her hair back behind her ears.

"So, no boyfriends to be jealous of?"

"Nope."

Her stomach tensed. How glad she was that Jasper wasn't coming to her mom's dinner tonight.

———

THE AFTERNOON PASSED in introductions with her mom, Jackson and Coop, who'd once more made the long trek from San Jose. Her mom was delighted. Sebastian's double cheek kiss hello and gift of perfume helped smooth the way, the latter also helping quash the niggle of concern about his financial situation. His gift to Ellie—another box of expensive-looking perfume—had drawn her own exclamation of appreciation. Sure, it was a little heavier than the light floral fragrance she usually wore, but his perfume—its very Frenchness—made her feel special, and more confident than she'd ever felt in her life.

She took Sebastian on a short tour of the ranch before he apologized and said he needed to have a rest before the party tonight. That was okay. She remembered the ravages of jet lag on her return. Plus, it gave her a chance to hear just what her brothers thought.

"Well?"

They exchanged glances then Cooper shrugged. "He seems nice enough."

"Because he *is* nice enough."

"Hey, don't get defensive."

"I'm not."

Cooper eyed her, smirking.

She rolled her eyes, glancing at Jackson who offered his own shrug.

"Hey, it's hard to tell when we've only just met the guy. Just remember you'll never really know what someone is like until you've known them for years."

And even then there were no guarantees. But no, she wasn't thinking about *him*.

"Look, I will say this: he's got a cool accent, and I can see why the ladies would dig him." Coop glanced at Jackson. "Is Lexi coming tonight?"

"I invited her." He looked at Ellie. "That reminds me. I also —"

"Oh, boys?" Mom called from the kitchen. "Would you mind getting those trays of vegetables in the oven?"

"You feeding an army, Ma?" Jackson said.

"Not an army, but it's always better to have more than less."

"For sure," Cooper said. "Hey, is Jess coming?"

"Did you invite her?" Mom asked.

"No." He looked at Ellie. "Hey, you don't mind if I see if she's free, do you?"

"Uh, sure." She liked Jessica Martin well enough, but the young veterinarian wasn't one of her closest friends. But then, Ellie's closest friend wasn't very close these days, either. A pang hit. She'd missed Jasper this week, but also still didn't know what to say to him, either. Which was why it was a relief to know he wouldn't be here tonight. She rolled her eyes at herself. Good thing she wasn't thinking about him.

As Cooper called Jess, Ellie busied herself with setting the table and helping her mom with last minute dessert preparation, while Jackson finished chores in the barn.

Later, Lexi arrived, which signaled the arrival of various other cars. Ellie set a plate of dips and crackers on the coffee table then tapped on Sebastian's door. "Hello? Sebastian? People are arriving. Have you had enough sleep?"

The door opened suddenly and she almost fell in. Then blinked at the sight of his bare chest before instantly pivoting her gaze to meet his smile.

"I missed you." His voice sounded as sleep tousled as his hair.

It had been an hour. "Did you want a shower?"

He lifted an arm and rumpled his hair, his bicep bulging. It wasn't as impressive as Jasper's—*stop!* "I've already had one. But I do want something else."

"Yes?"

"You." He tugged her inside, then wrapped his arms around her, his hands sliding up and then down, inching closer to her bottom as his mouth met hers. But she couldn't concentrate on the delightful sensation of his kiss as shock at his boldness mingled with concern that someone might see them. She pulled away. Fanned herself. Found a smile. "You better put on a shirt. I can hear another car arriving."

"I love kissing you," he murmured, his voice low and husky.

She traced a hand down his bristled jaw. "See you out there soon."

He nodded, pressed a kiss to her palm, then closed the door.

She exhaled, straightening her clothes as she hurried to her room, where she fixed her make-up—her lipstick, at least—and patted cool fingers on hot cheeks in an attempt to cool her flush. Wow. That kiss was nothing like Jasper's effort last weekend.

Ugh. She *really* needed to stop thinking about him. She splashed more perfume on her throat and wrists, and feeling newly bold, and desirable, and for once in her life, beautiful, she exited her room. Tonight would be amazing. She couldn't wait to show him off.

Then she moved to the hall, her excitement spilling out in a smile which dropped away when she saw who had just arrived.

Jasper.

———

SHE GLANCED across the table at him. As if they were connected his gaze flicked up to meet her then instantly away. She exhaled unsteadily as her stomach wrenched within. So far she'd managed to avoid talking to him—so mature, she knew—and had hung back when Cooper had done the introductions. But the sight of him had caused heart palpitations, and creased dread across her stomach. Not because of any fear of a repeat action from last Sunday, but because negotiating their relationship now felt more slippery than ice. She couldn't find the words to fake that things were all right.

Who'd invited Jasper? Probably Jackson, thinking she needed yet more brotherly protection. If only he knew she needed protection from his friend. Which meant Jasper hadn't told him. That was fine. The fewer people who knew the fewer people she needed to pretend in front of. And after this week, she was tired of pretending. She glanced at Sebastian. At least with him she didn't need to pretend.

Even if she had been taken aback by the forwardness of his

kiss. And the way his hug earlier had seemed a little handsy. Nope. It was probably just her being paranoid, or overly innocent. Look at her, twenty-five and never really been kissed, then she gets kissed twice—no, three times, now—by two different men in the space of a week. Rhonda Ingalls would call her a hussy. She reached across to hold Sebastian's hand.

He lifted her hand to his mouth and pressed his lips to her skin, which instantly earned an "aww" from several women. A quick peek across saw Jasper instantly avert his gaze, his jaw throbbing as if he didn't like what he saw. Her heart clenched. Well, good. Maybe he'd get sick of it all and leave.

———

He had to leave. Being here, watching Ellie and Sebastian smile at each other, the possessive way Sebastian slung an arm around her, felt like a show he had zero desire to watch. He glanced at Jackson, catching his eyebrow lift at the latest Gallic press of lips to Ellie's hand. Ugh. So clichéd.

He'd been an idiot to come. Yet Jackson's insistence, and his own sick desire to see what kind of man Ellie actually preferred, had hauled his butt here. Even though he'd known it was a bad idea.

The one good thing was that Ellie hadn't spoken to him. Had barely looked at him. Which left him free to look at her and feast upon her features. She looked so pretty, so happy. His heart wrenched, and he ducked his head again. He really should find a way to leave.

Except leaving would only announce to the world that he wasn't happy. So staying might help convince people he was okay, just like Jackson had said.

Ugh. He hated that Jackson now knew he had the hots for his sister. But at least in Jackson knowing that, he felt a little like there was one person on his side. Even if all the women here seemed to have fallen straight into swoony adoration for the guy with a French accent.

Jessica, the town's young veterinarian, nudged him. "So, what does the best friend have to say about this?"

Nothing that should be said aloud. He faked a smile, and shrugged. "She's a grown woman. She can choose who she likes."

"I do appreciate a man who recognizes that."

Yeah, but it wasn't Jessica's appreciation he wanted. Her gaze pierced him, and he was grateful when Cooper soon stole her attention.

He stared at his plate, at the smear of gravy decorating it. He should go. He'd definitely need to leave before dessert. But maybe he could help clean up so he didn't have to spend his evening avoiding looking at the woman sitting opposite.

"Are you finished?" he asked Jess. "Can I take your plate?"

"Oh, thank you." She handed it to him. "Let me help."

"No, don't worry."

He stood and glanced at Mrs. Reilly. "I'll deal with your plates."

"Oh, you don't need to do that."

Oh yes, he did. "Thank you for such a delicious meal."

His words prompted a flurry of thanks from the other guests. Apart from the man who was the guest of honor, who kept whispering in Ellie's ear.

She glanced at Jasper and he pivoted away, moving to the adjoining kitchen area and placing the plates on the counter. He opened the dishwasher, emptied out a few water-spotted plastic containers and dumped them in the dish drainer. Then moved the plates to the sink, plugged it up, then half-filled it, using the dish brush to wipe off the worst of the residue before placing each plate in the dishwasher. The Reillys had always talked about the importance of preserving water. Many years of visiting had taught him the value of this system.

"Hey there Cleaning Man." Jackson. "So, what do you think?"

"About?"

Jackson chuckled. "Yeah, he's coming on a bit strong, huh?"

He shrugged, staying focused on his task. If that was what she preferred…

"He's got Ellie wrapped around his finger."

Jasper pressed his lips together and continued his task. Scrape, rinse, load, repeat.

"I don't know…"

Jasper paused. "Don't know what?"

Jackson exhaled. "I saw her go into his room."

He froze. That didn't have to mean anything.

"Then come out with smeared lipstick. Sebastian wasn't wearing a shirt."

He spun to face his friend. "Why are you telling me this?"

"Because I think we need to pray."

Praying was about all he'd done all week. That, and worry. And work. And gnaw his nails. "Maybe you need to have a big brother talk with her."

"Oh, I will, don't you worry."

"Have a big brother talk with who?" Ellie said. Her eyes widened as she saw Jasper, and she placed a stack of plates down. "You."

"Ellie." His voice was raspy.

Her gaze narrowed. "So, has my big brother had a talk with you yet?"

"With Jasper?" Jackson asked, his gaze swinging between them.

"He doesn't need to. He knows."

Her eyebrow hitched.

Jasper shrugged. Jackson knew enough, anyway. Jasper wasn't about to advertise his kiss. It wasn't necessary. There was no point now, anyway.

He faced the sink, his shoulders sagging. Just a few more minutes and then he could escape.

A waft of strong perfume preceded Ellie's arrival by his side where she dumped the stack of plates in the sink. He inched aside, but still the fragrance irritated his nose. The perfume was cloying, heavy, and reminded him faintly of paint fumes. "You don't smell like you."

Ellie's eyes flashed. "I happen to love it."

"He gave it to you, huh?"

She cast him a look that could wither spring leaves and swept past him, only to return a moment later with a fancy-looking bottle and made a point of looking at him as she sprayed it on her wrists. Then she departed again.

Jackson's whistle sounded behind him. "I don't know what you've done to tick her off, but she's mad at you."

A niggling feeling suggested things might not go well for him should Jackson find out from someone else that he'd kissed Ellie. But still, admitting that felt too raw, especially now, when she was with the man she obviously preferred.

"Hey, if it's all the same with you, I might leave the rest of this."

"I'll help," Lexi's soft Australian accent said behind him. She placed a hand on his back, and he could almost feel her compassion burn through his shirt.

"I need to go." He blinked hard then turned, not meeting either gaze. "Tell your mom I said thanks. I'll go out the back way."

He grabbed his jacket and escaped. From the room, from the house, from the ranch. But not to home. Instead, he parked at the lakeside park, where the lights glimmered on a moonlit Lake Wainscott. And he folded his arms on the steering wheel and bowed his head as stupid, stupid moisture escaped his eyes.

# CHAPTER NINE

"So what do you think?" Ellie asked Sebastian, gesturing to the field where the football players ran up and down.

"It is not what I thought of when I imagined a small American town."

No. An Australian Rules football match—Aussie rules—held on the last Saturday of April was certainly a point of difference in Trinity Lakes' favor. But with all the Aussie expats who had moved here over the years, it shouldn't be that surprising that they'd want a taste of home. But she could understand how a Frenchman could find it weird.

Matt Kennedy leaped into the air, kneeling on the back of an opposing player, and grabbed the ball. A cheer went up from the spectators.

"Hmph."

Ellie glanced at Sebastian. He hadn't done a great job at disguising his reluctance to be here. But then, she supposed the quirky charms of Trinity Lakes—like this week's Anzac memorials to remember fallen soldiers, especially those from the Australian and New Zealand Army Corps—couldn't hold a candle to the bright lights of Seattle or Spokane. Still, she'd promised to take him to the latter soon. He'd appeared relieved by that, even though she knew going to the city would mean forgoing yet more museum work.

She returned her attention to the game but without really seeing anything. Olivia Darcy would be mad. Already Ellie could see how it wouldn't take much for some of these balls of responsibility she was juggling to come crashing down. She'd had several more phone calls requesting bookings for the ranch stay, thanks to the enthusiastic review Marnie had posted on Instagram. That had necessitated a juggle of time zones to speak with Mindy and Cooper. They'd now hashed out a more effective booking system that could be directly linked with their marketing. The phrases they kept using had been enough to fry her brain, but she'd tried to sound like she knew what they talked about. She bet Jasper would know.

She ducked her head as shame crept over her. She shouldn't have been so rude to him last Saturday. Put it down to tiredness, or feeling off-balance by sensing she was being judged by everyone. And there had been extra weirdness knowing Jasper liked her enough to kiss her, then parading a new man in front of him one week later. How exactly was she supposed to negotiate that? She still hadn't even come to terms with Jasper's no-longer-hidden affection, let alone how to balance that with a man who made his affection hungrily plain.

A shiver wracked her. Last night's kissing session had made that very obvious, and she'd had to pull back and tell Sebastian to keep his tongue in his own mouth. But even so, there was a thrill there, something dangerous that could easily flame to wanting more. She'd been so grateful when Mom had walked into the living room, forcing Sebastian back to his seat to pretend to watch the movie.

She exhaled. Maybe her brothers were right to be cautious. Sure, they along with everyone else had done their best to make Sebastian feel welcome last Saturday. And yes, while it had been satisfying seeing some of the young ladies this week observing her with what looked like respect in their eyes, she sensed her brothers didn't like him too much. She'd seen the way they'd rolled their eyes when Sebastian had pleaded tiredness as an excuse not to go to church last Sunday, then they'd arrived home to discover him on their home phone, chatting to someone in French. She didn't mind. She understood jet lag better than her brothers did, but she had wondered if Sebastian knew how much international phone calls cost. Her French wasn't good enough to understand much of what he said. Maybe he was just missing home.

But there had been a couple of moments when Sebastian hadn't seemed to understand she couldn't drop everything and devote herself to his entertainment. She'd tried to make sure she took him to interesting places, like Joe's Diner, and the Bellbird Café, and the Country Club. It was silly of her to worry. He was a city boy, so of course he wouldn't understand that horses still needed feeding, that stalls still needed mucking out. She'd appreciated his understanding in coming to Trinity Lakes this morning while she did museum things. He'd looked around briefly before she'd encouraged him to look through the Village Shoppes Emporium. Hey, if a girl had signed up to help a museum reopen then she actually needed to be there occasionally for that.

A cheer from the sidelines broke through her memories, stealing her attention to where a man was being patted on the back, as the scoreboard reflected another six points being added to the USA team. She joined the applause then paused. The man in the sleeveless striped top and shorts that showcased his muscular build was Jasper. She hadn't realized he would be playing today.

"He kicks well for an American," Lexi Franklin said with a teasing grin.

Ellie nodded. There was a reason a number of NFL teams

used Australian-raised kickers in their squads. Jasper's shorter height and muscled frame wasn't the lanky, lean body type usually associated with Aussie rules. But he had always been good at kicking in American football, so he must be a ring-in, brought in to boost the numbers. That must be why he'd left the museum early today. She'd not spoken to him, had barely dared look at him, but she'd noticed the instant his truck had roared away. Her eyes burned anew, and she blinked away emotion.

A glance at Sebastian showed his slow clapping cease before a bored expression stole over his face. She really should be doing more to make his time here enjoyable.

"Do you want to go to Walla Walla tonight?" she asked.

His expression brightened. *"Oui."* He gestured to the field. "I confess I do not understand the rules. It is not like real football."

"Real football?" He knew NFL? "Oh, you mean soccer."

"Do not call the beautiful game that. That is an abomination to the ears."

She laughed. Sebastian's fun sense of humor was what had drawn her to him. He made her laugh, just like Jasper. Only now the thought of Jasper only seemed to bring her to tears.

———

JASPER GLANCED behind him as Ellie's laughter floated across the field. His gut tensed, his fingers clenched. He returned his attention to what his captain was saying. Thank goodness his regular basketball games meant he had the fitness to play, especially with all the running and leaping this sport required. It felt like a long time since he'd played in any football game, Aussie rules or otherwise.

But still he couldn't concentrate. Could only think about what the Euro-god was saying that made Ellie laugh. Was he treating her right? Being a gentleman? His fingers clenched tighter as he fought to squash mental images of them kissing. But she probably loved kissing Sebastian. How could she not, when Sebastian was her choice, and Jasper wasn't? His heart ached.

"So that's clear?" his captain asked.

Clear as mud. But it probably didn't matter. It wasn't like today's game meant anything beyond modest bragging rights for another year.

He'd been glad for the extra practices this week. He'd needed something to distract him from the pain that threatened to swallow him whole. Having a week devoted to training and trying to get his muscles to remember how to play had proved effective distraction, exhausting him so much he'd crashed into bed each night and gone straight to sleep.

But even in the midst of sleep Ellie begged for his attention, stealing into his dreams, teasing him with her smiles and laughter before morphing into that woman of last week whose flashing eyes and scorn shriveled his every pore.

He trudged behind Logan Wylde and the others. He was supposed to be standing—guarding—his man, Joel Manning, from the ball.

"Who is Ellie's new dude?" Joel asked.

"A guy from France."

"Ooh la la." Joel curled an imaginary mustache.

Jasper shrugged, eyes on the play as Peter Franklin, today's referee, bounced the ball. Then a ruckman tapped it out, and there was a scramble of arms and legs as the opposing players tried to punch the ball clear.

"You jealous?" Joel asked.

"Of what?"

"Well, the dude's not exactly ugly, is he? And that accent?" He winked. "You might need to keep an eye on her."

"She's a big girl. She can manage." And she'd made it clear she wanted nothing to do with him, avoiding him at church last week, at the museum today, not even meeting his gaze. He'd broken things completely. "Besides, Jackson's around. She's his sister."

"I always thought you two were—"

"Nope."

"But don't you want to—?"

"Nope."

Never had he ever been so glad to see a ball flying toward them which necessitated his running into position, dodging Joel as he hurried close, before grabbing it to take a solid mark on his chest. Then he had a free run to line up the tall white goal sticks, take aim, and kick.

Yes. He fist-pumped as it sailed through the center two of the four poles, accepting the congratulations of his teammates, before glancing back to where Ellie had stood before. But there was no smile that lifted his soul, or cheering, or applause. He swallowed. She'd already gone.

———

"AND THAT'S WHY, when we talk about Anzac Day, I think it's a wonderful opportunity to consider the sacrificial love of Jesus. Love that persists, love that seeks another's good above its own." Peter Franklin smiled. "Let's pray."

Jasper bowed his head and closed his eyes as the guest preacher's words wrapped around his heart with gentle conviction. Lexi's dad's message about soldiers laying down their lives for each other was an excellent parallel to that of Jesus. How much of Jasper's love for Ellie was selfish and self-seeking? He wanted her to be happy, right? He probably needed to try a bit harder, then. And even if she didn't want anything to do with him, then that'd be okay. He'd be patient, he'd wait until she was ready to talk. He'd been in his own head too much lately, consumed with worries, and that wasn't helpful. It was time to make more of an effort. Including with the man she'd chosen over him.

"Amen."

He echoed it a second later, glancing up to where Ellie beamed. A suave looking Sebastian smiled beside her, his teeth looking like they'd never met a cup of coffee, as she introduced him to congregation members.

Jasper's heart wrenched, but he pushed past it. If he truly meant that prayer it meant he was going to change. Which meant doing things differently. Like talking to Sebastian. He frowned, then caught himself. *Sorry, God.* Hey, if God loved the dude, then it meant Jasper had to try to like him. Or talk to him, at least.

He pulled himself up, his body protesting with unfamiliar aches and pains thanks to yesterday's game. He'd never been so tired or so grateful to clamber into bed last night and drop instantly into sleep. He didn't know how older guys managed, but the fact they did meant he wasn't going to complain.

"Good morning, Jasper."

He smiled at Mrs. Franklin and inched his way around to where Ellie and her admirer had a bevy of adoring fans.

"Good game, Jasper," Peter Franklin said, stretching out a hand.

"Thanks." He shook his hand. "It's been a while. I'm feeling it today, that's for sure."

"None of us are getting any younger."

He nodded, thankful when Peter's attention was claimed by someone else, and his gaze could sneak back to Ellie and Sebastian.

Ellie glanced up, met his eyes. He tried for a smile but it wouldn't come so he settled for a nod instead. She ducked her head.

Okay, so she didn't want to look at him. That didn't bode well for talking. Still, he maneuvered his way past others to join them. Only to see Ellie slink away. Huh. What could he do to make things up to her? He got that it was awkward, but this was getting ridiculous.

Sebastian glanced at him, an eyebrow lifting.

Jasper found a gritted-teeth smile and stuck out his hand. "Hey. We met last weekend. Jasper Cohen."

Sebastian nodded, and clasped Jasper's hand for a second then dropped it. "You were playing that game yesterday."

"Aussie rules? Yeah. It was fun."

"It did not make sense to me at all."

Okay. "It takes a little time to figure out the rules, but I guess the same is true of any sport."

"Hmm." Sebastian's attention was stolen by an older woman who wanted to reminisce about her visit to Paris last century. Jasper stuffed his hands in his pockets, waiting for his chance. He'd heard stories of people who considered some Europeans rude, but had figured that was likely due to cultural differences. However, Sebastian's shifting stance to almost block Jasper from inclusion seemed ill-mannered. At least it left him free to look for Ellie. There she was. Talking to Mrs. Darcy and Georgia. Probably talking museum stuff again.

Did it make him a fool that he still wanted to help Ellie with that? Or was that just a case of him seeking her good above his own?

"You wanting to talk to him for your sake or someone else's?" Jackson murmured behind him.

"Dude." He shook his head. "I'm making an effort. That's all."

"More than what he's been doing," Jackson muttered.

Jasper refused to bite. He couldn't afford to get caught in the vicious cycle of hating on the man he barely knew. "Hey, remind me. When do you take Brutus on his stud duties?"

"On Wednesday. I'm back Saturday night. I hope every-thing'll be okay." His brow lowered.

Jasper couldn't get into it, his heart hovered too close to hurt to be impartial. He shifted the topic to sports, including hockey, now into playoffs, which Mitchell's team had made this year.

Jackson shrugged. "He's as confident as ever, but you know. There's only ever one winner in love and war."

Ain't that the truth?

"Sorry Jasper, do you mind if I steal Jackson?" Lexi said, with an apologetic grin. "We're having lunch with my parents. I'm sure you could come. You could bring Ellie like last time—oh." Jackson's pointed finger at Sebastian saw her nose wrinkle. "I forgot. Well, you'd still be welcome anyway."

"Thanks, but I have plans," Jasper said.

"And I'm pretty sure I heard Ellie say something about driving up to Spokane."

"Today?"

Jackson shrugged, and when he spoke his voice was low. "He wants to sightsee, she wants to please. They can drive there and get back. It's only two and a half hours each way."

"Only, he says." Lexi rolled her eyes.

"She's got other commitments, so she's gotta fit it in where she can. And speaking of other commitments, by the look your mom is giving us, Lexi, we'd better scram."

"See you, Jasper."

"Dude." Jackson fist-bumped him and followed Lexi through the thinning crowd.

Leaving Jasper still waiting for Sebastian to acknowledge him.

He glanced across at Ellie, still listening to Mrs. Darcy. She'd need to wind that up soon if they were going to have any meaningful visit in Spokane. Not that he cared. Not that he *minded*, he told himself firmly.

He edged around, stepping into the gap and giving Sebastian a nod as he continued talking about France.

"…yes, my family has a vineyard in Burgundy. We visit as much as we can."

Jasper's eyebrows pushed up as his heart sank. "Your family owns a vineyard?"

Sebastian shrugged. "It is not a very big one, but it serves our needs."

"Your need for wine?" Jasper tried to joke.

Sebastian stared at him, his upper lip curling, then glanced back at Mrs. Baxter. "I do not understand why people here are so strongly against it." He waved at the stained glass decorating the window. "Even Jesus turned water into wine, so why does everyone drink grape juice?"

Good question. But Jasper wasn't prepared to get into such questions, even if what Sebastian said surprised him by making sense.

Fortunately, Ellie came over at that point, smiling politely at Mrs. Baxter, her eyes skating past him. She clutched Sebastian's arm. "Sorry to interrupt, but if we're ever going to make it in time we need to leave now."

*"Oui, ma cheri."* Sebastian wrapped his arm around her.

Jasper stifled annoyance. Did the guy act like that because of his French-ness or because he knew of Jasper's own stupid feelings? Had Ellie said anything to Sebastian about Jasper? She still didn't look at him. Seemed to be looking everywhere else, instead.

Still, he had to try. Had to try to show he wasn't a bad guy. That's what love demanded, putting her feelings above his own. So he'd make one last effort.

"Well, in that case, I guess we should be saying *Ciao.*" He internally face-palmed himself as Sebastian's curled lip drew up into a definite sneer and he muttered a disparaging-sounding French word Mrs. Baxter didn't hear.

Mrs. Baxter laughed, patting Jasper on the shoulder. "I think you mean *Au revoir,* dear."

Way to go, looking like an idiot. If he had any questions why Ellie preferred the suave and smooth European model-like dude, he'd just gone and put his foot in his mouth and made it plain. This standing here pretending he didn't hurt was excruciating, paining him more than any sport he hadn't played in years.

"Have fun," he said.

But they'd already turned away.

# CHAPTER TEN

"So the main building of the Bible college was originally built in the late 1800s by the Heathwood family, before it was sold and turned into a home for abandoned illegitimate children in the early 1900s. One of those boys was adopted by some rich Christians with relatives in Australia without children."

Ellie looked over the pictures, studying the black and white photographs that Peter Franklin was showing her. Several days ago Peter had brought a new and unexpected aspect of the museum to her attention—the inclusion of the sizeable Australian connection to the town. The craziness of the past few days hadn't permitted conversation with Peter until now. She sipped her coffee from the Bellbird Café—another of the Aussie influences—and blinked hard to stay awake. Not that his information wasn't fascinating, but she'd been running on empty since her way-too-late return from Spokane on Sunday, and even though it was now Saturday, she'd been playing catch up ever since.

Peter flipped open an old journal, the leather cracked and

creaking. "Jodie found this in the college's library. It had slipped behind a bookcase, but we thought it such a treasure."

She reached to touch it then paused. "May I?"

He smiled. "It's not the Book of Kells. You don't need white gloves."

"Still, it's an important artifact."

"It's important to us at the college, but whether it's of enough interest to others." He shrugged. "It's why I wanted to show it to you to see whether you thought it was important enough to include."

She touched an ink-smudged page. "We have some letters and old diaries and journals. But those are mainly from some of the older families in the district." Like some of her own family's photographs from a century ago. "It would be wonderful to have something that really helps explain the Australian link a little more."

Peter nodded. "Well, this certainly does that." He tapped the opened page. "Here Henry Bellamy writes about returning to Trinity Lakes when he was an older, successful, godly business-man, and seeing the building and being faced with all these memories. He wrote about wanting to make it a place of life, not fear, abandonment and death."

"How wonderful," she murmured.

"He decided to make it a Bible college with the hope of creating a safe place for Aussie young people in their gap year to fulfill their dreams of traveling, while at the same time building strong foundations of faith."

Her heart panged. Sure, she'd traveled, but she hadn't exactly been shining Jesus along the way. Thoughts of how she and Sebastian had been kissing lately intruded, convicting her yet more. Did Sebastian even believe in God? But asking for God's opinion on her relationship with Sebastian felt like a huge risk. What if God said no?

"Anyway, his own son was tossing up whether to travel or go

to Bible college at the time." Peter's voice intruded into her thoughts. "It seemed a perfect answer to anyone in the same position. Parents were happier to support their young adult children's travel plans knowing they were going to a safe, supportive place where there were many Australians and where they would strengthen their faith."

"That's awesome."

"So that's how the Australian connection began with the Bible college, which helped shape the connection with Trinity Lakes. From what I understand, it was then further reinforced when locals James and Marianne Kennedy spent five years in Australia. They taught at a school in a small country town where their five children went to school. When they returned to Trinity Lakes and started working in the local high school, James introduced Australian rules football to the gym program. Marianne introduced the Anzac story into the World War One history classes, and the Australian Anzac festival was birthed several years ago."

Ellie nodded, peering more closely at the journal. "Perhaps we could get some photographs of this, especially the most pertinent pages, and enlarge it to include in a display. That way the college could still keep it in their possession. I'd hate to think something might happen to it here."

"I'm sure it would be safe. But I can understand your point." He gestured to the table behind him. "I did manage to find some building plans of the original house, which I thought might be of interest."

"Absolutely." She joined him at the table, poring over the design as her mind whirred with information about how to incorporate this into a six by three feet display case.

Already she'd had Marianne mention some other iconic Australian items she had lying around at home. Things like jars of vegemite, round tins of Arnott's biscuits decorated with brightly colored Australian flora and fauna, retro-looking canisters of tea. Her mind kept ticking. Perhaps they could have a short video of an AFL game that people could watch and listen to the rules if they pressed a button. Excitement sparked. That'd be awesome. But how to get the technology to do so? Maybe tech-head Cooper had a friend who might know.

She wrote herself a reminder then thanked Peter for entrusting her with the journal to do with as she needed. She promised to take excellent care of it and placed it on the desk in the office before going back to her scribbles from before. She sketched out another design that might incorporate some of these photos of the journal, and the memorabilia.

Around her the sound of industry continued. It was now three weeks until opening, and while some of the workers had dropped away, others still showed up each week. Like Marianne. Like Shona. And Jasper.

Her heart panged with regret. The childish way she'd been treating him pursued her through the crazy juggle of chores, chasing her to sleep. And yet he kept showing up at the museum, kept bending his back to whatever task was listed on the whiteboard, kept nodding toward her whenever she accidentally glanced his way. It was like he was waiting for her to make the first move, lest he frighten her away again.

And that was the thing. Now that she'd had more experience, she recognized his single kiss, though unexpected, had held respect. Sebastian's kisses? Not so much. Sometimes Sebastian seemed consumed by something other than love, and she was growing tired of his constant whispered demand for more. What kind of guy asked a woman to prove her love for him in that way? Conviction clanged. If only Sebastian's kisses didn't possess the power to weaken her knees and make her feel special and desirable instead of plain old Ellie. Still, she'd see if she could get Sebastian to come to church again tomorrow.

———

HE DIDN'T COME.

The church service drifted past her ears as she sat wedged between Mom and Jackson, conscious there would be people wondering about the absence of her flirty French friend. How to explain he'd been complaining again and called her an innocent when she'd slapped away his wandering hand last night on the couch? As it was, she'd found his murmurs of wanting to go away with her were getting harder to refuse. Sure, she had commitments, like the museum, that made it hard to jump up and go on a mini vacation. And she could understand that a man used to cosmopolitan life might find Trinity Lakes a little dull in comparison and want to see more of the USA. But the thought of traveling anywhere with him made her wonder just what he'd expect. Like whether he'd want to save money by sharing a hotel room. And a bed.

She shivered. Last night she'd been impossibly glad when her brother had returned from his trip escorting Brutus to do his studly duty. Surely Jackson's presence meant Sebastian would be less likely to come knocking on her door in the middle of the night. Bile swam. At least he knocked.

"Amen."

Theo Ladan had finished? Oh. She joined the others in standing, then had to make a quick getaway. Sebastian had claimed tiredness for not joining them, but she sometimes wondered if he was growing tired of her as well as their small town.

"Ah, Eloise."

She turned, found a smile. "Hello, Mrs. Darcy."

Olivia nodded to her, drawing her aside as the congregation talked around them. "Now my dear, I have to say, it's good to see the museum is coming along well, but I was thinking it perhaps needs a teensy bit more attention if we're going to open in three weeks."

Ellie nodded. Olivia Darcy's comment was not news. She'd

suspected as much, but when a visitor from France demanded her attention—and her kisses—a girl had a hard time saying no.

"I'll be there each day," she promised Olivia.

"I hope so. It is not a good look for certain sectors of the community to see the director missing in action."

Ellie winced. "I'm sorry. It's just we have a house guest—"

"I well understand the demands of a house guest, but I'm sure I don't need to remind you of your contractual obligations."

Her very soul seemed to cringe. How humiliating to be brought to task like this.

She blinked back emotion, offered her assurances to Olivia again, and ducking her head made her way outside to her car, swiping at tears.

What was she going to do? The more time she spent with him the more she knew things couldn't keep going as they were. The way Sebastian's hands slid to caress her made her uncomfortable. And the way he kept hinting at making things permanent—maybe finding a job at the nearby ski resort, or working at a restaurant—meant he was seeing this far more seriously than she was. Even if he wasn't serious about some things like she was. Like church. He'd come once, after the excitement of the Anzac Day Football match, before again pleading last night's late hour for not attending today.

"I don't understand why you have to go," he'd murmured against her ear. "It seems so old fashioned."

She'd heard that phrase a lot in recent days. Her reluctance to French kiss—Jasper had been right—had seen Sebastian accuse her of old-fashioned values. Trinity Lakes also earned a patronizing smile and murmurs of quaintness, which she suspected leaned more toward strange than charming. And while she still liked him, liked that someone so sophisticated chose *her* and made her feel special, the fact he often complained when she had chores or museum obligations was growing tiresome. Not that she'd admit that for the world. Even if she felt a little trapped. She wiped at her cheeks. But how could she get out of it?

"Ellie?" Jasper's voice. "Are you okay?"

She stilled, not facing him. How could she, when she'd barely seen him since that awful night of Sebastian's arrival? Well, she'd seen him, usually at the museum on Saturdays when his work ethic put hers to shame. Or on Sundays at services. Each time their eyes met he'd nod then look away. She hated how she'd been treating him, understanding his confusion when he'd apologized but she'd ignored it. Even his opinion on the perfume Sebastian had given her had stuck, and she wore it now because she resented Jasper's comment rather than because she loved the scent. But she hadn't spoken to him, nor he to her. Until now.

"Ellie? Please. Can we talk? I thought we were friends."

Friends.

She'd thought that too. Until he'd kissed her. And while she still hadn't reconciled that part of their relationship with all she thought she knew, the fact he still wanted to pursue friendship with her, even after her coldness and rejection, made her turn, and dare to meet his gaze.

The concern in his eyes filled hers, forcing her to blink away more stupid, stubborn tears.

"Aw, Ellie." He took a step toward her, then stopped.

But she was already moving, wanting, no *needing*, his arms around her.

And when she slammed against his chest, and his arms folded around her, and she whispered a "sorry" against his chest, for a moment she felt like everything could be okay again. For a moment she dared relax into his comfort, his safety, his assurance.

Until a voice said "Ellie? What are you doing?"

————

JASPER FELT her stiffen in his arms in the second before she drew away.

"Sebastian!" Ellie's chin lifted. "What are you doing here?"

He shrugged. "What are you doing here with him?" He scowled at Jasper.

"It's not what you think. We were just in church, and—"

Sebastian dropped a French word Jasper was pretty sure was blue. But Ellie's brow only creased. Maybe she didn't recognize some French swear words like Jasper now could, having recently looked up online what Sebastian's comment last week actually meant. The guy was so wrong for Ellie but telling her wouldn't help any. He was tempted to tell Jackson, but Jackson had been away this past week and probably didn't need to be bothered concerning this the instant he got home. But there was something not right about the Frenchman.

His internet search had sparked another for information about the vineyard Sebastian's family owned. He was glad for Google translate, but even with that help it was hard to find out more.

"You are supposed to be with me, not him."

Whoa. Possessive much?

"She's not with me," Jasper clarified. "She was upset, and—"

"Oh, *ma* Ellie." Sebastian cradled her face in his hands and kissed her, long and passionately.

Jasper wasn't sure if it was for Ellie's benefit or for Jasper's, but the kiss seemed to go on for a long time, long enough to crush his spirits. She seemed to be enjoying it, enjoying him, and that just made his heart sore.

By the time they came up for air and Sebastian slung a possessive arm around Ellie's shoulders he was wearing a smirk. "I have things under control now."

The word waved like a red flag. That was part of the issue.

Jasper didn't trust Sebastian and had never liked the word 'control' being used in a relationship. He'd always thought Ellie was wise enough to recognize when she was being manipulated but perhaps emotions got in the way of being able to see clearly. He understood that. He hadn't felt like he could see clearly ever since she'd gone away.

"We'll see you later," Sebastian said, steering her away.

Jasper caught her apologetic glance, and the way she asked Sebastian what he was doing when he'd said he was too tired to come to church today. He didn't catch the Frenchman's reply.

Jasper's hands clenched. His gut burned. There was something clearly shady about the dude, but saying so to Ellie wasn't gonna win him any points. Worse, he might even get accused of racism. But then not saying anything meant letting the bad dude win.

*Lord, what do I do?*

Everything felt so precarious now, like one false step could send him back to Antarctica again. He closed his eyes, praying for calm, and the memory of her in his arms filled his mind again. It still seemed impossible that she'd hugged him. Yet his pores seemed to sizzle in memory, and traces of her fragrance still lingered on his collar.

Had she really said she was sorry, or was that a figment of his imagination? She might not have said anything beyond that, but at least it felt like there was a glimmer of hope, which was a surprising amount more than what he'd woken up to this morning.

"Lord, you need to help us out here. If there's something wrong about the dude please expose him. And keep Ellie safe."

The crunch on the parking lot's gravel behind him suggested that other church members were exiting. He rubbed a hand over his face and nodded to Mrs. Franklin and Jodie before two familiar faces loomed before him.

"Dude." Jackson frowned. "What are you doing out here?"

"Leaving?"

Lexi's red-gold hair swung over her shoulder. "Are you okay? You look a little… lost."

"I'm fine."

Lexi bit her lip, like she wasn't buying it, but she didn't press him. Bless her.

"Hey, have you seen that sister of mine anywhere?"

"Yeah." Jasper's voice was flat. "She left with Sebastian five minutes ago."

"Sebastian came to church?" Jackson's voice was incredulous. "I thought he hated it."

"Ellie was surprised."

Jackson exhaled. "I hate to say it, but there's something about the dude that I just don't trust."

"Jackson." Lexi placed a hand on his upper arm.

"Sorry babe. But it's true. It's a bulldust meter we guys have, where we can tell if another guy is lying. You feel the same way too, right Jasper?"

He glanced at Lexi, offered a nod.

"It's not that I don't trust my sister, but we barely know him."

Exactly. "What's his last name?"

"Kuhl," Jackson said.

"Cool? Tell me you're kidding."

"No. K-u-h-l. I think it's of German origin. That's what he said once. Why do you ask?"

Jasper shrugged. "He just mentioned some family vineyard and I was curious to see where that might be."

"Huh. First I've heard of it."

"What *is* his job?" Lexi asked. "It seems unusual for a man to take so much time off."

"People travel." Jackson frowned. "Except he hasn't done much of that, now I think about it. Which is weird."

Totally weird. But still, he shouldn't leap to conclusions.

"Maybe he just wants a break in the countryside." See? He could offer reasonable doubt.

"It's an awful long way to come from France just to see the countryside."

"But not if he's in love with your sister," Lexi pointed out.

Jackson exhaled heavily. "And he does seem to be doing that. They're always kissing—"

Talk about a dagger to the chest.

"—and then last night, I thought I saw him try her door."

"What?" Jasper's pulse thundered in his ears.

"It might've been innocent, but then it might not have been also. And I don't like the fact he's in our space."

"Can't you kick him out?" Lexi asked.

"He's Ellie's guest, so it's a bit delicate."

"Can you talk to your mom?" Jasper asked.

"I can talk to her," Lexi offered. "I'm sure she'd want to do all she can to keep Ellie safe."

Jackson winced. "I don't want to make this more of a mountain than it might be. So let me talk with Ellie, then I'll talk with Sebastian, and we'll see. I could have the guy completely wrong, and maybe it's just a cultural thing."

"Yeah, I don't know." Jasper kicked the ground with his boot. "Look, I might be biased, but there have been a few things he's done that make me concerned." He mentioned about the swearing, the word 'control' which widened Lexi's eyes and caused Jackson's to narrow. "And then he's off doing random stuff." He shrugged. "I don't wanna go poking my nose in where it's not wanted but I think you need to keep an eye on him—and on them. Call me crazy but I don't know what a sophisticated French dude hopes to gain by hanging out in a rural part of the US."

"But Ellie is so sweet," Lexi protested. "I can understand a man finding her attractive and wanting to get to know her. Just because you've known her all your life doesn't mean another man mightn't be attracted."

"It's not that."

"Nope." Jackson's mouth pulled sideways.

"What?" Lexi looked between them. "What are you not telling me?"

"Nothing, hon. Nothing to see here at all."

Lexi frowned, then glanced back at Jasper.

He tried to paste on coolness, but maybe it was too late as Lexi gasped. "You like her."

Jackson held up his hands, surrender style. "I swear I didn't tell her."

Jasper hissed out a breath. Captain Obvious had just made things even more plain.

"Jasper." Lexi's eyes held such sympathy he had to look away. "I'm so sorry. I didn't know. How long has this been going on?"

He shrugged, shoved his hands in his back pockets. "It's not going. Obviously."

She placed a hand on her throat. "You and her would be perfect."

His mouth twisted, along with his heart. "Yeah, well, it's one thing for you to think that, it's another for her to feel the same way."

"I'll be praying that she does. Soon."

Emotion clamped his throat.

"Better pray that her eyes are opened to all kinds of things," Jackson said. "If Sebastian is as shady as Jasper seems to think, then she needs to be kept safe."

"You're around this week though, right?" Jasper asked.

"Yeah." He nodded. "I'll talk to Mom as well. Maybe let Coop know he could head this way for another visit sometime soon too."

"You're a good brother," Lexi said, smiling up at Jackson.

Jasper's chest knotted. How he yearned for the day when Ellie might look at him with similar admiration.

But he'd wrecked that. Had lost the right when he'd kissed her without permission. And proved that best friends didn't make the best sweethearts. Or any sweetheart at all.

Still, the sermon today had reminded him that God was in the redemption business, and that with Him, anything was possible. And what Jasper needed now felt like a miracle of the exceedingly, abundantly, above all he could ask or imagine kind.

He sucked in a breath and pushed out a tight smile. Good thing God was into those kinds of miracles too.

# CHAPTER ELEVEN

"Are you serious?" Ellie stared at Jackson in disbelief. "How can you even ask me something like that? I don't know whether to laugh or be insulted."

"Hey, I'm just looking out for you."

"Is that what you call it?" Her eyes narrowed. "Did Jasper put you up to this?"

"What? Why would you say that?"

She stilled. Why *would* she say that? He'd been nothing but considerate, nothing but concerned. She shouldn't be projecting her guilt on someone else.

"Look, Jasper mentioned that he's heard him swear in French."

"Jasper? He doesn't know French," she scoffed. "He said Ciao the other day."

Jackson's lips twitched. "Regardless, I'm just saying that we're concerned. And you should be careful. And if Sebastian is making you feel uncomfortable, then you only need to say so."

"I can take care of myself."

"I know. But you might want to be careful about what signals you're giving him."

"How dare—?"

"And keep your door locked at night," her brother continued ruthlessly.

"What?"

"I'm pretty sure I saw him trying your door last night."

She stilled. So someone *had* been there. She shivered.

"You don't know much about him, and I don't want to see you get hurt. So please, be wise. And if you want help kicking him out—"

"Jackson!"

"—then I'm more than prepared to do so." He crossed his arms. "I'm here for you, sis."

His words touched her, but she still had to keep up the protest. A sister couldn't admit her brother was right, could she? "Look, I appreciate the fact you're looking out for me, but you're getting carried away." Although she still didn't like how Sebastian had virtually dragged her away from Jasper, then insisted on showing her how much of a man he could be, kissing her until she'd had to pull away, begging him to stop.

"But I can't stop," he'd complained. "You make me crazy."

It was a heady feeling thinking that plain her could make a man crazy. Her lips twitched. Maybe that's what had happened to Jasper too.

"This isn't a laughing matter," Jackson complained.

"I'm not laughing."

"You smirked, and that's virtually the same."

"I wasn't smirking about that," she protested.

"Then what were you smirking about?"

Trying to explain how she was stunned that Jasper might've liked her once upon a time seemed too fraught with challenges to easily explain. "Let's just say that I will take your concerns to heart and be careful."

His shoulders slumped. "I appreciate it."

"You're not my dad, though, so you don't get to tell me what to do."

"I know that, but consider this as me caring."

She nodded. "You haven't said anything to Mom, have you?"

"Nope. And I don't intend to. She's got enough on her plate."

"Good."

A tap came on her door. "Ellie?"

"Man. He doesn't like to leave you alone, does he?"

"Some might call that caring," she snapped.

"Some might call that control," Jackson countered.

"Like who?" she challenged.

"Jasper."

Jasper. Her heart sank. After years of being treated as a tomboy and being boyfriendless, it was awful being in this position. She didn't want to be someone a man was jealous over. She wanted to be someone a man could trust.

She stilled. And she wanted to be with someone like that too.

———

HER WEEK PROGRESSED MUCH like the previous, except with Jackson back in the house it felt like she could breathe easier. Conscious of what she'd promised Olivia she made time each day to work on the museum pieces, coordinating collection dates with Marianne Kennedy, and working with Hallie Holloway at the college library to photocopy Peter Franklin's journal.

Most of the exhibits were coming together, the glass display cabinets from the previous museum space had all their contents removed, dusted and replaced. They'd been moved as well, so now there was more continuity in how the historic pieces were displayed in chronological order.

So now, after the admission desk, the visitor would be taken to the new Native American exhibit, complete with some artifacts of bows and arrows discovered locally. This led to the revamped Lewis and Clark display now bolstered by a covered wagon, complete with a special cook wagon, which had been in the back in a storeroom. Wheeling these out on display seemed far better than letting them sit in storage gathering dust. Then came the exhibits displaying more memorabilia from some of the early pioneering families, like the Gilbertsons and the Reillys. Pride filled her to see the old photographs of the ranch in its early days, before the big red barn was built. Recent rabbit trails of research had led her to discover a site devoted to preserving Washington's old barns. And while their barn might be considered a little young, she was glad to know there were people committed to preserving the heritage of such things.

After the pioneer section they would have the first of the world war exhibits, followed by the Roaring Twenties, then the case committed to the Depression and Dust Bowl of the 1930s. The Second World War exhibit was followed by the new display honoring the Australian heritage of Trinity Lakes, then the Vietnam War, then the exhibits committed to more modern events. Visitors would gain a good sense of what constituted Trinity Lakes' history. And with the more interactive displays—like the video of Australian sports (for which they still needed the technology to run), and a dress up corner where people could don historical clothes and hats—she hoped visitors would find it fun as well as informative. The latter idea had been a suggestion from Mindy, who'd said they could encourage people to take photos in front of a sign displaying the hashtag #LoveTrinityLakes which could help garner online traffic. The clothes had been donated from one of the recycled clothing vendors at the Village Shoppes Emporium, which would get its own little placard mentioning their generosity.

So many of the local businesses had proved so supportive. Not least of which was Cohen's Hardware, whose generous donations of supplies and skillful laborers had transformed this place from dingy to delightful. She owed Jasper so much.

"Oh my."

Ellie's head snapped up. Olivia Darcy stood at the door with Georgia beside her. Both wore big smiles. "I cannot believe it," Olivia said.

"We've been working hard." Ellie moved toward them. "It's not quite finished, but Jasper and some of the others have been busy moving things into position." Following her instructions on the whiteboard. She wasn't sure how Jasper managed to fit in helping her when he was so busy with paying clients, but her gratitude was enormous. And try as she might, she couldn't help but compare this to Sebastian who refused to acknowledge her busyness as legitimate. This, and his insistence on her taking him places, made her question whether his affection was primarily focused on the physical. Her heart knotted. Just what had she gotten herself into? Maybe if she just held the line, she'd find a way of getting untangled from something she was starting to dread, and she could—

"Well, I must say it is remarkable the way you've managed to get things looking so much more finished in just a few days."

"We're nearing the finish line, but there are some things still to finalize." She told them about the idea for the video and the dress up corner.

"I love that," Georgia said, pointing to the corner. "You're thinking of having it over there?"

"Yes."

Georgia's face brightened. "If you had enough clothes from different eras, you could maybe theme it. Like have a colonial frame where people take photos behind, or one with a fifties or sixties vibe."

"What do you mean a frame?"

"You know, like a photo booth at a wedding when people have their selfies." Georgia shrugged. "It wouldn't be hard to create some. Then we could take some nice pictures for the Trinity Lakes Gazette."

"Oh, but I couldn't ask Jasper to make them. He's given up so much time already."

"He *is* a fine young man," Olivia said. "So community minded." She glanced at Georgia. "You think it's hard to find a suitable young man at the university. Well, there's at least one right here in Trinity Lakes."

Ellie's mouth dropped open. Did Georgia like Jasper? Why that hurt her heart she didn't want to explore. Georgia was young, but she was mature for her age, and these days held an understated elegance about her that made her even more attractive. Ellie frowned. Georgia might've grown up next door, but she'd always seemed pretty quiet, more invested in her photos and music than connecting with people. She and Liam were close—Ellie supposed that's what happened when parents died —but Ellie's efforts to befriend her more deeply had always been stymied by her work commitments on the ranch.

Olivia moved to inspect the new Native American exhibit, leaving Georgia to wait with Ellie. She glanced at her watch. She really should be getting home soon.

"You don't need to look like that," Georgia murmured.

"Look like what?"

Georgia's mouth curved up on one side. "Like I'm going to steal your favorite toy."

"Excuse me?"

"Jasper."

Indignation rose. "He's not my toy. I don't treat him like a toy."

"Sorry. No offense meant."

"Do people really think that? Who's said that?" How awful people thought that of her—of him!

Georgia shrugged. "People have said you've got your fancy French boyfriend, and yet Jasper is still hanging around."

"You heard your grandmother. It's because Jasper is a good guy. And we're friends. That's all."

Georgia nodded. "Well, you don't need to worry about me. Ignore what Gran said. I'm not looking for a man. And if I was, I'd be picking someone who wasn't in love with someone else."

Ellie's cheeks heated. How could people think such things? "You're wrong. How many times do I have to say it? Jasper Cohen and I are only friends. And that's all we'll ever be."

———

JASPER STILLED, then swung immediately back out the way he'd come in. No way was he going to let anyone see him, see his heart break. He'd wondered—hoped—that Ellie might finally be seeing him differently, with that whispered sorry against his chest, but maybe that was for something else. Like taking him for granted these past weeks.

He moved to his truck, leaned against the bed. Maybe he deserved to be taken advantage of. He'd proved himself a fool regarding Ellie in so many, many ways. But still this stubborn belief that they were meant to be together refused to die. That if he just gave Sebastian enough rope he'd trip up. He kept praying the scales would fall from Ellie's eyes. He didn't know what else to do without coming across as the jealous, scorned lover.

"God, what do I do?"

The blue sky above didn't echo with a booming voice from heaven. Instead, inside his heart he felt the faintest whisper that he return to the hardware store. So, after dropping off the supplies, taking care he wasn't seen, he drove back.

Once inside the store he stopped beside his dad, who was stacking paint cans. "Dad, you really shouldn't be bending down like that. Get one of the other workers to help you."

"I don't need people fussing," his father said. "I've done this for years. I can manage."

"Let me." He picked up a can but his father brushed his hand away.

"How many times do I need to tell you I've got this?"

"Fine." He backed away, pointed to Jordan and gestured for them to keep an eye on his dad. Jordan nodded, and Jasper moved to the office.

He sank into his chair. Stared at the computer. He really should be dealing with invoices, but persistent worry refused him that luxury. Instead, he found himself looking up vineyards in France, specifically for a Kuhl vineyard in France. When that didn't come up with any answers he searched for Kuhl winery, wines, vines, and all related search terms. Still nothing.

Weird. He then tried all kinds of combinations for the name connected to the wine industry. Still nada. Then did a search for Sebastian Kuhl.

Whoa. No wonder the dude looked like a model. He actually was one, according to this site. He had to use Google Translate to understand, but it seemed Sebastian had done some work in magazines and was represented by an agency in Milan. Or, he squinted harder, he had been. This was from two years ago. So did that mean Sebastian still was a model or was he now working in a winery like he'd implied?

It felt weird to be looking up Sebastian online, and he sure hoped nobody came in and saw him looking at all these pictures of a half-dressed man. But the more he searched the more questions he had. What exactly did Sebastian do for a job? Was he one of these influencer types who basically sold whatever to the highest bidder?

If so, he had to be on social media. He moved to open Instagram—the store had an account, but Jasper had never felt the need to create a personal profile—and yep, sure enough there was photo after photo of Sebastian, but none of Ellie. Huh. What was that about? But maybe this was a professional account, designed to get noticed by agents or agencies. It probably helped to give the impression he was single and looking for a good time.

Next he switched to Facebook, and after more careful sleuthing, he scrolled through the dude's Facebook account—he hadn't set his photos to private— and found a few photos of Sebastian and Ellie. His heart clenched at the ones of them both smiling at the camera, Ellie's face holding a joy he hadn't seen in weeks. Maybe these were old photos.

He kept scrolling. Sure enough, there were plenty of selfie pics of Sebastian, on his own, with famous European landmarks in the background. Whoa—with a beautiful woman who wasn't Ellie. When was this taken? He squinted at the date. New Year's Eve. So, before he'd met Ellie. The escalating anger was forced to subside. He hadn't been cheating on her back then. But it still didn't stop the questions on Ellie's behalf. What did she really know about Sebastian?

Jackson had his concerns, and while a guy could be a model —he supposed that was a legitimate career choice—the fact he'd said nothing about it raised red flags. Had he said nothing because he thought it was pretentious to talk about modeling? Did Sebastian think they would judge him? Well, they probably would. In fact, Jasper already had. Didn't need the model tag to do so either.

Before he fully realized what he was doing his fingers were tapping out a message to Jackson. *Did you know the guy is a model?*

*Which guy?*

He tapped back. *Ellie's guy.*

His heart hurt looking at those two words. Sebastian wasn't supposed to be Ellie's guy. Jasper was.

"Jasper?" Dad called from the other room.

"Give me a minute, Dad."

He glanced at his phone. Jackson's latest message had pinged through. *I thought he worked in a winery.*

Yeah, Jasper had too. *Maybe it's time to ask him point blank*, he typed back.

His fingers clenched. It was way past time to ask that question.

"Jasper."

"I'm coming, Dad." He glanced at the computer screen, his lip curling. The guy obviously couldn't be trusted. And the fact he was somehow exploiting this situation with Ellie made him so mad. He scrolled back further, then saw a post that opened his eyes wide.

Seriously? Was that the reason he'd latched on to Ellie?

"Jasper!"

A clattering sound and Jordan's voice snagged his attention. "Yeah?"

"It's your dad! He's fallen and isn't breathing."

"What?"

He rushed from the office to see his father, not ten yards away from the office door, clutching his right shoulder as he lay motionless among a collection of spilled paint cans. "Dad!"

He knelt by his side and looked for a pulse. "Has anyone called 911?"

Jordan held his cellphone to his ear, rapidly rattling off information.

"Get the defibrillator," Jasper shouted, before beginning chest compressions.

*No. No!* His eyes filled. But he had to stay calm. Had to remember the training from last year. Lexi's actions in saving Jordan from drowning had prompted numbers of townsfolk to undertake training in CPR and use of a defib machine. He wished he remembered it now.

How could he have ignored his dad while searching for evidence about the shady boyfriend of the woman he loved?

*God, don't let my failures kill my dad.*

# CHAPTER TWELVE

There had to be more to life than this. Ellie shoved another shovel of horse manure into the nylon bag. The glamor of Paris had never seemed so far away.

From beyond Brutus's pen she heard voices. Jackson was talking to Denny, the foreman. She paused, fork in hand, and eavesdropped. Anything had to be more interesting than this.

"…says he's a model."

Who?

Denny said something she couldn't hear. Then Jackson muttered, "Here he comes now."

"Pardon, have you seen Ellie anywhere?"

She shrank into the shadows. Once upon a time she'd felt strong enough to handle Sebastian herself, but now she felt exhausted, ill-equipped mentally or physically to stop him. He was so demanding, chewing up her energy even when he wasn't around. She definitely couldn't be around him now. Besides, she *really* wanted to know more about what Jackson had been saying about Sebastian.

"I haven't seen her for a while," Jackson said. "Maybe she's still at the museum."

"*Non.* Her car is here."

"Then I can't help you man. But hey, you can always help us. There's always plenty to do around a ranch."

Sebastian laughed, like he thought Jackson was making a joke. Except Ellie knew her brother, and he wasn't.

"I will see if I can see her somewhere else."

After a second, there came a cough. "Yeah, you wouldn't want to earn your keep or anything would you?" Jackson muttered.

Her eyes widened. Jackson was right. Sebastian never offered to help. He'd never once offered to help around the ranch or the museum. He never did anything he didn't want to do. Instead, he'd gladly used their hospitality, even driving their cars without so much as asking, like he'd admitted to last weekend when he'd randomly shown up at church. She'd never realized just how much he focused on himself, like he was wanting to be the center of attention, having people work their days around him. Like they were the slaves she'd joked about with Jackson all those weeks ago. How selfish was he?

He'd also never paid her back. She, and the rest of her family, had basically bankrolled the man for his entire stay here. Even when they'd taken trips to Spokane she'd ended up paying for gas and meals.

Had he just been using her? Abusing her family's generous hospitality? She certainly felt used. Thank God she'd never given him more than kisses.

She shivered, recalling last night when Sebastian had found her alone. Mom and Jackson were both out at Bible study, and she'd been left wondering whether she should have found one too. But Sebastian's murmurs of returning to France with him, to see his family's vineyard, to live there, had caught her by surprise.

"You want me to visit you?"

He'd wrapped her tighter. "I want you to live with me."

"Live with you?" She blinked. "I couldn't. I can't."

"You can. People do it all the time."

"But not me." She drew back, pushing away his arms. Honestly, the man was like an octopus. "I would've thought by now that you understood that I'm not that kind of girl. I'm not living with any man unless I'm married to him."

He smiled. "Well, we could do that then."

"What?" Was he serious? "Sebastian, I don't know what to say. Apart from that's insane."

"Is it insane to want to marry the woman I love?"

Her heart hiccupped. "Did you just say love?"

"*Oui.*" He smiled. "I love you, *ma cheri.* And I want to spend forever with you."

Her head was awhirl. Her heart, too. "This is too much. I don't think you know what you're saying."

"I know exactly what I'm saying. And it doesn't have to be hard. We could go to Las Vegas and be married tonight."

Married? She'd laughed it off, but the man's intensity had freaked her out to the point that she'd not dared breathe a word to anyone. Imagine if Jackson knew. He'd be pulling out the shotgun and making sure Sebastian fled Trinity Lakes for good.

And truth be told, she'd be kind of glad if he did, because she had the feeling she was entangled in something and couldn't escape.

Regret kneaded her heart. How could she have ever thought Sebastian cared for her? How could she have left God out of this? Tears pricked her eyes. *Lord, I'm sorry. I should've talked to You about this, and I didn't. Sebastian isn't who I thought he was, and I ran ahead and didn't listen to those—like Jasper—who tried to warn me about this. Please help me get out of this mess.*

She took a breath as some of the knots released. God, who loved her more than anyone, would help her. She sensed that, no, *knew* that now. Now if only God could help her with the situation with Jasper, too.

How could she have ever thought Jasper inferior to Sebastian? She'd been a fool, a blind, stupid, too-innocent fool, caught up in the headiness of her first real romance and drug-like kisses without realizing the lack of character behind the man. In every way Sebastian was the lesser man to Jasper. Every way. Jasper's goodness and patience and kindness was everything she truly valued.

Her heart thudded. Jasper *was* everything she wanted. He was way more than just a friend. He was the man of character she could—she wanted to—build a life with. Build her future with. How could she have treated him this way? Would he even want her, after she'd wrecked things so badly? And now she had to get out of this mess with Sebastian, and somehow fix things with Jasper so he'd know how she really felt. But first, she needed to get rid of Sebastian. *Lord?*

The sense to speak to Jackson grew. She moved to find him and finally own up to the truth when her phone rang, and she snatched it up. She couldn't afford for Sebastian to learn where she was, especially now when she had no idea what she was going to say to him.

She frowned at her phone's screen. Why would Lexi be calling her? Wasn't she at work today? "Lexi?"

"Oh, I'm so glad you picked up! Look, I don't know if I'm supposed to be doing this, but you need to come to the hospital. Jasper's dad has had a heart attack and is in the emergency room. Jasper is here, and I think you need to be here too."

"What?"

"Gotta go. Pray." The call ended.

No. *No, no.* Mr. Cohen was the dad she'd never had. He *had* to be okay. Oh, poor Jasper. Poor Jasper! She had to see him. Now.

She stripped off her gloves and hurried from the barn, Fido scampering at her heels.

"Ellie?"

She paused. It was only Jackson. Phew.

"What's going on?"

"It's Jasper's dad. He's had a heart attack and is in the emergency room. I'm going there now."

"I'll drive you."

"No, it's okay. Keep running interference for me."

"With Sebastian?" He grinned. "Gladly."

"I owe you."

"He owes all of us. Big time."

She nodded. That was for sure.

She raced to the house, praying she wouldn't see Sebastian. She found Mom, told her what had happened, and begged her not to tell Sebastian.

"Because?"

"I just need to be there, not have him hovering all the time. I can never be myself when he's around."

Her mother eyed her. "You've only just figured this out?"

Ellie scrubbed her hands, splashed water on her face. "Why has nobody said anything?"

"We thought you liked him and that you were happy." Her mother stroked her cheek. "But you haven't been happy with him for a while now, have you?"

Her eyes filled, but she didn't have time for explanations. Any minute Sebastian might appear and then she'd be held up even longer. She hurried to her room, stripped off her t-shirt and jeans, and exchanged them for clothes that didn't smell like poo.

She grabbed her bag, her phone, her keys, pausing as her mom caught her attention.

"Please pass on our prayers, and tell Jasper that I'll make a lasagna and drop it off to their place later."

Ellie kissed her cheek and raced out the door, ignoring Sebastian's shout behind her as she slammed the car door and raced out the drive.

All the long drive to Trinity Lakes she kept praying. For Mr. Cohen, for Mrs. Cohen, and for Jasper himself. Oh, poor Jasper. She needed to see him. Needed to apologize. Needed to tell him how she felt.

The lakes glimmered blue in the sunshine, but she paid them no heed. "Lord, heal him, give them peace. Help them."

By the time she pulled into the hospital parking lot she was a sweaty mess. She hurried inside, saw Lexi who was triaging another patient. Lexi pointed to the hall. The hospital wasn't large, and Ellie knew the waiting area Lexi meant. It was the waiting area used by all relatives of patients in the hospital.

She skidded to a standstill. Mrs. Cohen was exiting the plastic doors and someone—Jasper—was going in.

"Mrs. Cohen?" She stepped hesitantly toward her.

"Oh, Ellie."

Ellie wrapped the older woman in a hug, and let her cry on her shoulder, each tear and jerked sob twisting further pain inside. Surely he wasn't dead?

"Oh, you'll have to excuse me." Mrs. Cohen pulled back, swiped at her damp face.

Ellie found a nearby box of tissues and handed her several.

Mrs. Cohen dried her face. "Thank you." She patted her face dry. "I don't know why I'm so emotional. He's alive."

"Oh, thank You, God."

"Amen." Mrs. Cohen shook her head. "I don't know what I would've done." She peered at Ellie. "How did you know?"

"Lexi told me. She thought you might need support. I told Mom and she's making you a lasagna and will drop it by your place tonight."

"Bless her. And Lexi. And God bless you." She grasped Ellie's hand.

Ellie squeezed it and led her to a seat. "Come on, let's sit down. Can I get you a cup of tea or anything?"

"No. Forgive me. I'm sure it's just the shock."

"So Mr. Cohen?"

"Is stable. Jasper is in with him now. They're only letting one family member in at a time."

"Do the doctors think he'll be okay?"

Mrs. Cohen nodded. "The doctor said if Jasper hadn't started CPR when he did then he mightn't have made it."

"Jasper saved his dad's life."

"He's a hero, my boy."

"He sure is." Her eyes filled. How could she have ignored the true hero for the one who merely looked good?

"He's always been a good boy. So faithful. So loyal."

Ellie wasn't sure if they'd switched from talking about Jasper's deeds as a son or something else. But it didn't matter. She was convicted enough right now. She knew the giant mistake she'd been so close to making. Her chin wobbled.

"Ellie?"

She swiped at her moist eyes but emotion kept roaring like a runaway train.

"I'm so sorry." She hid her tears in Mrs. Cohen's neck as she hugged her. "So sorry."

Sorry for what had happened to poor Mr. Cohen. Sorry for all she'd done to poor Jasper. "It's such a mess. He'll never forgive me."

Mrs. Cohen stroked her back. "I think you'll find he's understanding."

"But that's the thing." Ellie pulled back. "I was taken by surprise when he kissed me, as I'd never realized he thought about me in that way."

Mrs. Cohen's eyes widened a little. Had Jasper never told her? Oh dear. But it was like her mouth had never heard of a bridle, the way words kept pouring out.

"And then I didn't know what to do about that and I freaked out a bit, and then Sebastian came and he was what I'd always imagined a dream boyfriend being like. Until he wasn't, and now I can't get rid of him, and I don't know what to do. But I knew I had to be here today, because you're like family. And Mr. Cohen is like my dad, the dad I wish I'd had. And Jasper is so dear to me, and I just want to say I'm sorry, to him, and to you, and to let you know I'll always be here for you. I love h—you all, and just wanted you to know that. And that I'm sorry."

Mrs. Cohen smiled. "I think he knows that."

"That I truly am desperately sorry? I hope so, because I never meant to hurt him. I've just been so confused lately, but now it's like things are clearer and I can see what's important. And honestly, Jasper is one of the most important people in my life, and I need to let him know that."

"I think he knows."

"How?" Ellie swiped at a leaked tear.

"Turn around."

Ellie winced and closed her eyes. One guess who stood behind her. But after putting him through the wringer these past weeks and making enough of a fool of herself already, what did more humiliation matter?

"Ellie."

Jasper's voice was raspy, but the tenderness there was enough for her to turn and face him, then run to him and put her arms around him.

"Oh, Jasper. I'm sorry. I'm so sorry."

---

JASPER HELD HER LOOSELY. Just like he'd had to do for so long in his heart. Then she tightened her clasp, burying her head in his neck, her lips against his skin. And as if his body understood forgiveness better than his heart did, he drew her closer, her words sinking deep into his soul. He was dear to her? He'd take it. But had she really said—or implied at least—that she'd broken up with Sebastian? His hopes jumped.

Her arms tightened. "I'm so sorry for having hurt you," she said again. "Please forgive me."

"Already done." His neck grew wet. She was crying? Aww, poor Ellie. Any remaining frost melted away.

"I don't deserve your friendship," she murmured.

Friendship? But from what he'd thought he'd overheard her say before…

His gaze lifted to his mom, whose raised brows and questioning smile said she'd thought the same. But hey, they had to start somewhere. Even if they had started this journey so many years ago, back when he'd been ten and Ellie had been nine.

"I might go check on how your father is doing," his mom said with a wink.

He managed a nod but didn't let go of Ellie. Now was the time to make things right, and the opportunity felt so fleeting, he had to do it properly.

"Hey, Ellie, it's okay. We're good."

She lifted a tear-stained face. "You forgive me?"

He smiled, stroked her cheek with his finger. "Always."

Her bottom lip wobbled then she tucked her head in the crook of his neck, her clasp around his torso growing in strength.

He didn't care who saw them. He closed his eyes, and savored the feel of her, savored this moment of restoration.

The other questions concerning Sebastian, her future, his future, could wait. Right now was all about forgiveness and the renewal of friendship. And if a future relationship was to ever happen, it would need to be built on something more certain than what their friendship had been in the past rocky weeks.

He exhaled, and the worries that had consumed him eased slowly. The doctor had assured him it wasn't that last bit of exertion that had caused his father to have a heart attack. He'd actually praised Jasper for his quick response and use of the defibrillator machine. Jasper shivered. Thank God they'd had that training last year and that he remembered it.

"How is your dad?" she whispered, as if she could see his thoughts.

"They say he's stable now, but he'll need to be on medications for probably the rest of his life."

"I'm so sorry this happened."

"Me too."

"He's such a good man."

Jasper nodded, his throat tight.

"Like you are," she continued.

Now he had to blink away his own tears.

"You're such a good man. And I've been so blind. And I don't know how you can forgive me, but I'm selfish enough to take it."

"I meant it," he murmured.

"See? You're such a good man. I don't deserve you."

Deserve him? His hopes flickered again. Did she mean deserve him as a friend? Or something more? He swallowed. "Ellie, I—"

Commotion behind them stole his words, and he glanced up to see a scowling Sebastian push into the space.

"Ellie, what are you doing?" Sebastian drew close, his hands fisted.

Ellie's arms tightened. Was she scared? Jasper rubbed her upper arm and shifted, bracing as he faced the French man. "My dad is sick."

Sebastian shrugged as if it didn't matter. It probably didn't, not to him.

"Sebastian, didn't you just hear Jasper? His dad is very sick. And his dad is important to me, and so is his mom, and I wanted to be here."

"With him?" He jerked a thumb at Jasper.

Jasper's grip tightened.

"Stop it. Jasper is my friend. My best friend. And I need to be here with him now."

"But—"

"You heard her, buddy. Now back off."

Sebastian muttered something under his breath, then exhaled loudly. "I would like to speak to my girlfriend alone please."

Jasper glanced at her, and she nodded. "I'll be right here." And he'd message Jackson to get here asap.

# CHAPTER THIRTEEN

"I cannot understand why you did this to me."

Ellie crossed her arms, braced her feet, glad for the support of Jasper not ten yards away. "I cannot understand why you are making this all about you. Didn't you hear me before? Jasper's dad is very sick. How dare you make this about you?"

"But you ran away when I called to you."

"Because I had to be here. What part of that don't you understand?" She frowned. "How did you know I was here anyway?"

"Your mom said so."

She had?

"She also said I could use her car."

Was he telling the truth? Sometimes it was so hard to tell when he looked at her with such sincerity. But then his actions clamored louder than his words. "I'm gonna call her to check."

"You don't trust me?"

No. Nor did she trust herself. She felt like he could manipulate her. Was this what they referred to as a gaslighter – someone who made her second-guess her thoughts and motivations?

"I don't understand you Ellie. I've come here to see you, I

want you to come back to France with me, to see my family and our vineyard. I want you to live there with me."

"I told you before. I can't do that."

"You could marry me."

She blinked. He hadn't been joking before? But it still felt unreal. And now that she knew what she did, her answer was even more clear. "I could, but I won't."

His smile faded, then hitched up again. "It wouldn't be too hard. We could go to Las Vegas—"

"You said that last time, Sebastian. And just how would we get there? On tickets I paid for, or would you finally pay for something?"

His mouth sagged. "I can't believe you think so little of me. Of course I would pay for you to be my wife."

Except she had the strangest feeling that she'd be the one paying for the rest of her life. Her chin tilted. "The answer is no."

"No?" He smiled. "You cannot mean that."

"I can."

"But I love you, *ma cheri*. And I want to spend forever with you."

She shook her head. "I don't think you do. I think you want someone to love you and pay your bills forever. That's what I think."

Sebastian blinked. "You cannot mean it."

Laughter behind them stole her attention to where Jasper now stood with Lexi, Jackson, and Mom. "I think she does," Jackson called.

Sebastian's beautiful face transformed for a second. She stepped back. Caught Jasper's scent before his arm caught hers, his arm around her shoulders completely different to Sebastian's controlling embrace. Jasper made her feel safe.

"What even is your job, Sebastian?" Jasper asked.

"I told you. I have a vineyard my family owns."

"Yet there's no evidence of that on the internet."

"We're a little vineyard."

"There is evidence that you used to do modeling."

"Used to? I still do."

"Yeah, not according to your agency."

Sebastian's eyes flashed. "You spoke to Miranda?"

"No. But I did see that you'd asked on Facebook how to get a US green card."

Ellie's breath hitched. Wait—had that been Sebastian's scheme all this time? Had he not wanted her, but had pushed for marriage because it would get him into the country? For his *modeling career*?

"I don't know what you're talking about," Sebastian said with a sneer. "You probably misunderstood, like you do so many things." He drew closer to Ellie, eyes on her. "What we have is special. Ellie and I love each other."

She ducked her head, emotion roaring through her ears. How could she have ever trusted the man? Even now she felt like a mouse caught in a cobra's trance. But one thing was clear.

"I do not love you," she said firmly. Maybe she'd been caught up in the idea of love—and yes, his handsomeness and kisses might've sailed awfully close to lust—but she knew she didn't love Sebastian. Not like she loved someone else.

"But you do. You told me you wanted to go to Las Vegas tonight."

Jasper's arm slipped from her shoulder. "Ellie?"

"I didn't say that. I would never say that." She glanced at her mom. "You know that."

"I do." Her mother turned to face Sebastian. "I also know you took my car without permission."

"But you told me I could."

"I did no such thing. You're lying."

"We're going to press charges," Jackson said.

"What?" Sebastian's face paled.

Ellie's mouth dropped. "Really?" How awful. And not just for Sebastian. All of her naivete would be revealed and talked about for years. Trinity Lakes was a haven for some gold-plated gossip mongers.

Jackson pulled his phone out, pressed some buttons. "I've got the local sheriff's number, and I'm prepared to call him. Unless…"

"Unless what?"

"Unless you leave Trinity Lakes and never return."

"But I love your sis—"

"Leave Trinity Lakes, and never return," Jackson repeated, lifting his phone to his ear.

"But my things are at the ranch."

He cared more for his things than her?

"I'll take you back. Then take you to the nearest airport." Jackson's voice and stance said he wasn't taking no for an answer.

"I do not understand all this negativity."

"Seems like not enough people have told you no in your life," Jackson said.

Ellie cringed. She should've said no more often. No to his kisses. No to his demands. No to him. Thank God she'd said no about the most crucial things. But still, she felt used, violated, as much by her own stupid imaginings as Sebastian's manipulations.

Her eyes filled. "I can't believe I was such a fool to ever believe you."

He looked away. "What can I say? I thought you were pretty, and obviously desperate for affection."

Her heart buckled.

"I think you should call Sheriff Thompson anyway." Jasper's voice was edged with growl. "He'll just do this to another woman somewhere else—"

But before they could do anything Sebastian turned and ran.

Jackson quickly followed, and Jasper put his hands on his head, glancing back at her as if wondering whether to join the chase too.

"You should stay," Mom said to him. "Jackson will sort him out. Your mother needs you."

"Whoa, thanks. I forgot for a moment there." Jasper glanced at Ellie. "Are you okay?"

She shook her head. She felt humiliated, like she would never be right again. All she wanted was to find her bed and huddle under the covers forever. But she had no desire to return home until everything Sebastian-related was moved out. How could she have been such a fool?

"She'll be fine." Mom wrapped an arm around her. "Tell your mom that David is in our prayers. But I'll look after Ellie."

"I'm sorry, Ellie."

She shook her head. There had been too many sorry things going on today. She needed to get away. "Please tell your mom I had to leave."

Jasper nodded, his bottom lip tucked in.

She couldn't look at him. Exhaustion weighted her bones. But she couldn't go home. She had no wish to see people. Where could she go?

Maybe she could find much-needed solace in the museum.

———

It was late by the time Jasper returned home. The hospital had left him exhausted, time with his dad left him feeling guilty. Sure he might've saved him, but he should've stopped him from going to work. Should've not let himself get distracted by Ellie and her dating woes. He scrubbed a hand over his face. Poor Ellie.

The look she'd given when she realized Sebastian had only wanted her for a green card. His heart broke a little more for her then. But her mom had soon taken her away, then Pastor Ladan had visited, and he'd been forced to stay listening to doctors and nursing advice and what his dad's health would mean for their futures, and now he barely had enough energy to get out of his truck.

He glanced at his phone. He'd switched it off earlier, following hospital protocol, and he was half tempted to leave it off. Who wanted to be bombarded by the news of the world and the stuff that didn't matter?

Everything that did matter had boiled down to three things: God, his family, and Ellie.

With a sigh, he reached across to switch it on. He should find out what was happening with her at least.

His phone lit in a blaze of notifications, and he peered at them. Flicked through. But there was nothing from Ellie. His heart sank. He shouldn't be surprised. She'd probably said all she needed to earlier, in that all-too-brief moment before Sebastian's theatrics had stolen attention. Speaking of, maybe Jackson had an update.

Jackson had left a message to call him, so Jasper did.

"Dude, how's your dad?" Jackson said without preamble.

"They're keeping him in for a few more days to run some more tests, but he may be out by the end of the week."

"That's good news."

"Yeah." He swallowed. "How's Ellie?"

"Oh man." Jackson sighed. "She went to the museum, but came home not long after. Spent the rest of the night in her room. There was lots of crying."

His heart hurt for her. "And Sebastian?"

Jackson huffed out a breath. "Don't get me started."

"What happened?"

"Talk about vindictive. When I got back, I found he'd let Brutus out."

"Out?"

"Like *out* out. Out in the fields where he's not supposed to go. We had to call Jess Martin to come sedate him."

"Wow."

Jackson sighed. "And that's not all. By the time I finally got that under control and could chase him again, we realized he'd stolen Mom's car and gone back to Trinity Lakes, speeding to the highway. Would you believe the loser then crashed Mom's car?"

"Really?"

"Then apparently he hitched a ride with Kyla. I don't know if that's a good thing or not."

Jasper laughed.

"What?"

"I love the idea of two narcissists riding off into the sunset together."

"Come on, she's not that bad. Who knows, she might even get him saved?"

Jasper chuckled, this time without amusement. "He sure needs it."

"Yeah." Jackson groaned. "Right now we don't know where he is, and he owes us for crashing Mom's car. We're definitely pressing charges now."

"Poor Ellie. She'll hate having all of this come out into the open."

"Hey, the guy played us all. But yeah, she's devastated. Thinks she can't trust her judgment with men."

And there went his hopes again. He closed his eyes, leaning his forehead against the steering wheel.

"She'll come around, Jasper."

"Yeah." She had to. *Please God.*

"I think she just needs some time to recalibrate and feel like she can manage. Her head's been all tangled up in romance for a while now, so it'll take a bit of time to get things sorted."

"I know."

A beat passed. Two. "For what it's worth, I think you're good for her."

"Thanks."

"And I can't wait until she finally realizes that."

"Mm hm." Jasper opened the vehicle door. He really needed to end this call.

"Hey, where are you?"

"At home."

"Mom left a lasagna there on the front porch."

"I see it. Tell her thanks." Finally, something other than hospital vending food to eat. He yawned.

"Okay, I get it. I'm boring you."

"It's been a huge day."

"Yeah. It has. I'm sorry man. I'll let you go. We're expecting Coop any second now."

"Coop?"

"Yeah. I don't know what's wrong with these tech companies. The dude gets more time off than seems right. But Mom called him, and he's coming up for the weekend for some family time. Get this: now his playoffs are done, even Mitchell is planning to drop by."

Jasper winced. Great. There went any incentive in going to see Ellie.

"It's Mother's Day this weekend anyway, so we're planning to stay close."

Mother's Day? He should do something special for his own mom. He'd been so busy lately he'd forgotten. "You guys need it."

"As do you. Praying for your family."

"Ditto."

"Thanks." Jackson ended the call.

Jasper studied the foil wrapped baking dish, scooped it up and opened the door.

The house was silent. Mom was still at the hospital. Theo

Ladan had said he'd drive her home, but Jasper needed some time to himself, to just think, to just be.

He deposited the meal in the fridge, sank into an easy chair, without turning on the lights. He didn't need to see. He didn't need to eat. He only needed quiet, space to hear God, to pray. For everything today had shown that life was fragile. That life could flip on a dime. That a person could plan their course, but God would direct their paths.

He prayed for Dad. He prayed for Ellie. Prayed for the business. Prayed for Mom. Prayed for Jackson. For Jackson's family, too. Prayed for Ellie again. Then prayed for himself.

That God would lead them.

That God would heal their wounds.

That God would show them what was next.

That God would have His way.

In everything. Even with Sebastian.

His fingers clenched. How he hated wondering just what that man had done to wound Ellie. Had he forced himself on her? Was that part of her regret? Part of why she'd said sorry?

His breath hitched, and he tried really *really* hard not to imagine her with Sebastian. But the image of them kissing was burned in his brain. And it really didn't take too much for him to think they'd gotten more intimate, especially with Sebastian's pushy ways.

His eyes blurred. Poor Ellie. "Lord, heal her."

And God heal him. And help him to fully forgive.

# CHAPTER FOURTEEN

After the trials of previous years when her mom had been so weak, it now felt funny to be celebrating Mother's Day weekend with her mom doing most of the work. But ever since Thursday's shocking revelations, Ellie's body seemed to have been hit with a double dose of jet lag-like flu, and after managing only an hour at the museum she'd needed to return home. She'd tossed her perfume in the trash, huddled in her bed, and basically sniffled her way through the past few days, including an interview with Sheriff Thompson. The only bright spots had been Cooper's arrival yesterday, and today's visit from Georgia Darcy. Georgia was also in town this weekend for Mother's Day, and had already heard about the dramatic exit of Ellie's boyfriend thanks to the magic that was the Trinity Lakes grapevine.

"I'm so sorry," Georgia said. "You don't deserve that. It's hard to believe such a schemer was behind that handsome face."

"Never trust the handsome ones," Ellie grumbled. "They always want something."

Georgia nodded and glanced away, as the room filled with unnamed tension.

"What is it?"

Georgia turned to face her. "Did Liam ever tell you what happened to me?"

"No."

Georgia chewed her bottom lip. "Look, I don't ever talk about this, but something about your boyfriend reminded me of a guy I used to know." Her nose wrinkled. "Do you remember Gary Wickley?"

"Wasn't he the horse groomer over at your ranch once upon a time?"

Georgia nodded.

"Then he had a thing for that young Australian girl, right?"

"Elissa's sister, Lydia. That's right." She studied Ellie. "He liked them young, because they were naïve and more willing to believe him."

"Them?" Who else—oh! Her heart wrenched. "Oh, Georgia. I didn't know."

"Evidently." Georgia's lips twisted. "Gary tried to take advantage of me, but I didn't let him, so then he tried to make me go to Las Vegas to get married."

Ellie's heart thudded. Just like Sebastian had tried with her.

"I don't know what would've happened if Liam hadn't stopped him."

"God bless good brothers."

Georgia nodded. "But what I should've done was report him to the police. I didn't want all the embarrassing fuss, and neither did Liam. But because Gary got away with it with me he tried it on another woman. And I've been kicking myself ever since for not being brave enough to tell someone." Her eyes shimmered.

Ellie reached across the couch to hold her hand.

"I… I felt like I needed to come and tell you that. I should've said something before, because I hate to say it, but there was something about Sebastian that reminded me of Gary. He seemed to be looking for the next person, or opportunity. I didn't want to judge, especially when I didn't know the situation. But apparently there was enough truth there. It showed me that women need each other to be brave, to tell the truth, to stop those men out there who are bad and manipulative. We need to speak up so they don't keep getting away with it."

Ellie nodded. "I will be speaking to the police again."

"I'm glad. Since going to college, I've learned a lot about our rights and responsibilities as citizens. And I think being a responsible citizen is more than just being aware of causes, but actually standing up and speaking out and doing things that make a positive difference in this world. Whether that's sustainable environmental practices, feeding the poor, building houses for the homeless, or fighting injustice."

"Sounds like you're getting a lot out of college."

"Elissa has been great, but she heads home to Australia soon to get things finalized as she prepares for the wedding."

"Exciting."

"Yeah. But it means I'll need to find a new roommate."

"Because the Darcy millions can't keep you there alone?"

Georgia's smile flicked. "More like I don't really like being alone."

"No man on the horizon for you?"

She shook her head. "I don't want a man just to keep me feeling safe. That's not what I imagine a relationship to be like."

"I'll pray your Mr. Right comes along soon."

"Thanks." Georgia's lips curved. "Speaking of Mr. Right, what's happening with Jasper?"

Way to go to make her feel her world had turned upside down. "Nothing."

"Nothing? Or nothing yet?"

"I can't just jump from one relationship into another."

"From what I've seen, along with half the town, you wouldn't be jumping. Just returning to the best guy this town has to offer."

*The best guy.* Yes, he was. "He's a good guy, isn't he?"

"Yes."

"Did you hear he saved his dad's life?"

Georgia smiled. "He's a hero, as well as good looking."

"And he's a solid Christian. He lives out what he believes."

Georgia nodded. "And he's very community-minded, working as he has at the museum." Her head tilted. "Or is that because he's very Ellie-minded?"

Ellie's cheeks heated. "He hasn't called me since Thursday."

"Have you called him?"

"I don't know what to say. I hate that I no longer trust my own judgment. And it's like I don't want him to be my rebound when I can barely trust myself anymore."

"That's natural."

Ellie stared at her. "How can someone younger than me sound so wise?"

"I'm studying psychology these days, so maybe that has something to do with it."

"What happened to visual design?"

"Art and photography are still my majors, but honestly, I'm loving doing these other subjects too." She studied her. "You should consider studying. My university in Seattle has a really good history program."

Her heart flickered. "I'd love that. But I can't just leave Trinity Lakes."

"You could visit on the weekends if you really want."

"There is that ol' issue of money, too."

Georgia nodded. "There are scholarships out there, though. And financial aid."

Ellie shrugged. "Maybe. But I really can't think about stuff like that right now. There are too many other things to think about."

"Like Jasper?" Georgia teased.

"Don't."

"You'll call him soon?"

She nodded. "I'll need to. Even if it's just to find out how his dad is doing."

"Good idea." Georgia glanced at her watch. "I better go. Gran is expecting me. Ever since she went to the Bellbird Café and tried their Eggs Benedict she uses my visits home as an excuse to visit again."

Ellie winced. "I'll need to call her and tell her why I wasn't there these past days."

"Hey, I'll make your excuses. And a woman is allowed to be sick sometimes, you know that don't you?"

"Yeah." She stared at Georgia, who really seemed so much older than her age. Gone was the shy teenager-like girl she remembered from only last year. University studies had done a lot to help her mature. "I'll walk you out."

She accompanied Georgia out, just as Cooper and Jess entered from outside, followed by—

"Mitchell!"

"Sis."

His brown beard tickled her forehead as she hugged him. "What are you doing here?"

"Our season is now done, and apparently it's Mother's Day tomorrow, or didn't you get the memo?" His gaze trickled to Georgia. Maybe it was Ellie's imagination but he seemed to straighten and instantly morph into swagger mode. "Hey, I'm Mitchell Reilly."

"I know. I'm your neighbor." Georgia held out a hand. "Georgia Darcy."

His mouth fell open, and he took her hand as if it was made of glass. "You look different."

"So do you."

He rubbed his bristly jaw, then seemed to realize he was still holding her hand as he quickly released it.

"You made it to seven games," Georgia said.

His eyebrows rose. "You follow hockey?"

"Liam has season tickets in Seattle." Georgia shrugged. "I get there sometimes."

"Huh."

Ellie exchanged glances with Jackson and Coop who both wore their own expressions that veered between amazement and smirks. But the idea of their buff and burly brother being enchanted by the delicate millionaire heiress from next door seemed absurd. But you never knew. Case in point: Jackson finding happiness with Lexi who had come from the other side of the Pacific.

"I'm going to go now." Georgia glanced at Ellie's brothers, her smile small, her demeanor calm.

As Ellie led the way outside she caught Mitchell's murmured "Wow. She's really grown up, huh?"

She smirked to herself. The dude had no chance.

After farewelling Georgia, she walked around the back to the barn. Jackson and Jess were deep in conversation, with Cooper listening in as if he could speak animal science too. He couldn't, but that didn't stop him from acting like he did, spouting off what little he did know whenever he could.

Fido accompanied her as she veered instead to the bunkhouse, opening the first room and checking it was still in order for the guests who were supposed to arrive tonight. She'd thought it weird to have someone booking Mother's Day weekend to come stay, but they'd paid for last night, even though they hadn't stayed. Everything looked in order, and Ellie would be sure to take on her mom's chore of cooking for the guests, as it was Mother's Day weekend.

She pulled the door closed then checked the other room. It looked in order too, even though it wasn't needed for another couple of weeks, when Memorial Day weekend would see the museum open. She closed the door, tugged out her phone, and sank into the Muskoka chair positioned on the porch. Studied the screen. She shouldn't have to second guess it. A simple enquiry about how his dad was doing was all that was required. But the issue at hand was whether it led to something more she wasn't sure she was ready for yet.

Here went nothing.

*Hey Jasper, I've been thinking about you. How is your dad doing? X*

She chewed her lip, studying the X. Too much? Or not enough?

Oh, this was ridiculous.

She pressed send.

———

JASPER'S HEART hiccupped as he studied the text.

*X?*

One kiss didn't mean much. One kiss could mean everything.

He heaved out a breath. Stop. He shouldn't focus on the kisses. Should focus on the message, the fact she'd finally contacted him.

He hadn't wanted to push. Hadn't wanted to make her worry. But he'd been praying she'd reach out. He glanced at his dad lying in the bed with the playoffs on TV, and tapped the phone's keypad. *He's doing well. Itching to go home. Watching hockey with me.*

Her answer was swift. *You're a good son, suffering like that for him.*

He smiled. *Right? I'm glad you can appreciate the sacrifices I make. How are you?*

*Okay.*

He frowned. *You sure?*

*Yep!*

Huh. He wasn't buying that. But before he could type anything her next message shot through.

*How is your mom doing?*

*She's okay. Dad's sister and brother are staying with us so she's thankful for all the food that friends and neighbors have dropped in. We'll be eating casseroles for weeks.*

*Let me know when you need a Trinity burger instead.*

*Always.*

Her reply took longer this time. *Tonight?*

His heart skipped a beat or two. Did she mean with her, alone, like a date?

Somehow this felt like more than an invitation for food. That it might hold the keys to a future he'd scarcely allowed himself to dream.

He glanced back at his dad. It was only polite to hang with his dad for the game. And Aunt Cindy had come all the way from Maine and they were supposed to catch up tonight. And while he *really* wanted to see Ellie, the past few days had shown the importance of family, that time was precious, and he really shouldn't blow off time with them.

He slowly tapped out his reply. *Can't tonight. Sorry. My aunt is in town.*

Her reply was swift. *Tomorrow?*

His heart skipped another beat. She was eager. Then his heart sank again. He typed: *The doctors said there's a chance Dad might have to go to Walla Walla tomorrow depending on how his testing goes.*

*He's in my prayers.*

*Thanks.*

*Let me know when you're free then.*

*Will do.*

He wondered whether he should sign off with his own *X* but decided against it. He'd much rather do that in person.

"You okay there, son?" his dad asked, with a crease in his forehead.

"Yeah."

He motioned at the phone Jasper still held. "Who was that?"

"Ellie."

His dad smirked. "Of course."

"I do get messages from other people too, you know."

"None who make you look like that."

"Like what?"

His dad waved a hand motioning to Jasper's face. "Like you've just been handed the keys to a treasure map."

He looked like that?

His dad chuckled.

"What?"

"So what's she said that's made you look so happy?"

He shrugged.

"No, don't give me that. I nearly died, so it's my right to know. What's going on?"

Jasper sighed.

"Like that is it?"

Man, his dad must be bored to be this persistent. Although he'd made a good point before. "I think she wants to go out with me. But I'm not sure."

His father beckoned for the phone. "Want me to read your messages?"

"No!"

His dad grinned, showing his tease. "Well, it's about time. Tell her she needs to treat my son with respect. No more hoofing off after foreign guys. Got it?"

"Sure, Dad. That'll go down real well."

"Give her a hug from me."

Jasper swallowed, just imagining hugging Ellie again. Already two days without seeing her felt too long.

"Then give her a kiss from you."

*X.* "Dad. We're just friends."

"No, you're not. You've both been heading to be a lot more than that for a long time. So stop kidding yourself and pretending you don't love her. Everyone knows you do."

Great.

"It's time you showed her just what a catch you are."

Jasper's lips lifted. "Well, it helped when you decided to make a hero out of me."

His dad chuckled again. "You're welcome." He pointed to the screen. "Now stop talking. I want to see if Parotti has it in him to score a hattrick against Edmonton tonight."

"Against Guillemette and Hansen? No chance."

He picked up his phone and placed it down again. He longed to see Ellie but family came first. But while the game drew his dad's attention, Jasper's thoughts were on a ranch on a hill not too far away, as he wondered what a date with her might mean. Had she meant a date? Or was it just a chance to talk?

If she did mean a date, should he pick her up? Call him a wuss, but he'd rather not face the brothers. Jackson had mentioned earlier that Mitchell was planning a surprise visit to see his mom and Ellie, and while Jasper wasn't exactly scared of the dude he had never felt comfortable around him. Given those long-ago warnings, he'd be real happy to avoid him now.

Especially when he and Ellie might finally have the chance to work things out.

## CHAPTER FIFTEEN

"Who was that?" Mitchell asked, motioning to the phone Ellie had laid on the coffee table. He'd muted the game during the commercials.

"Jasper." She lifted her chin.

"He's still sniffing around, huh?"

"He's still my friend, if that's what you mean, yes."

"Friend, or...?" He lifted his eyebrows suggestively.

Her cheeks heated, and she was conscious all her brothers were staring at her. "I don't know."

"Yeah, that sounds like more-than-friend to me. Well, good."

Wait. "What?"

Mitchell shrugged. "You deserve someone who is the real deal, and he is. Good luck to him. And to you."

"Um, thanks?"

"What?" He glanced around at the siblings. "Why are you all looking at me like that? I'm not some big scary ogre."

"It's just you always have 'Opinions'," Cooper said, using air quotes.

Mitchell huffed. "Like the rest of you don't."

Jackson tilted a look at Ellie, then glanced back at Mitchell.

"Look, we all get that you're a famous hockey star, but some-times it comes across that you think that means the rest of us aren't quite on your level."

"That's stupid."

"Yeah. We all think so. But it's nice that you now realize that too."

Mitchell looked around as those seated in the living room burst into laughter. "What?" When nobody answered, he shrugged again. "Anyway, is there any more word on the French dude?"

Jackson's jaw tightened. "The sheriff said Kyla's car was found at SeaTac. A camera spotted them on a flight to Las Vegas."

Ellie blinked. "Kyla—and him? I can't believe it. She always seemed so sanctimonious."

Jackson shrugged. "Maybe she just wants to feel loved."

Ellie's head lowered. She knew now how a girl could get caught up in those kinds of feelings.

"So they could be anywhere." Coop shook his head. "I still don't get how you let him get away."

Jackson bristled. "I had to make sure Brutus was safe, considering he's an important financially contributing member of the ranch."

"Says that like he prefers Brutus to his own brothers," Mitch muttered.

"Some days I think it's true." Coop swapped glances with Ellie.

Jackson's chin rose. "Look, not everyone appreciates a know-it-all sticking his head into other people's business."

"We know that," Coop said dryly. "You made that abundantly clear last year."

Back when Jackson had finally admitted needing some help getting the ranch's finances back in the black.

"Have you talked to Sheriff Thompson yet?" Coop asked

Ellie.

"Yesterday morning." Mom had taken her in Ellie's car. Her cold meant she should've been in bed, something Sheriff Thompson pointed out, but she'd wanted to get it over and done with. And it had proved every bit as excruciating as she'd feared, owning up to her naivete, detailing her mistakes. He'd explained the Feds would likely need to be brought in, given Sebastian's nationality, and that he'd been spotted in Las Vegas, and that Ellie would likely need to do more interviews.

The sheriff had shaken his head. "You're lucky the guy didn't steal from you."

Yes, they were. How could she have been so trusting?

Her eyes had filled and his had softened with compassion. "Not everyone is trustworthy in this world, Ellie."

She'd nodded. She knew that now.

But the thought that people would pity her, perhaps secretly mock her for her naivete, made her long to hide away.

"Game's on," Mitch said, unmuting the remote.

The game continued, Vancouver versus Edmonton, in the second round. But while she could appreciate the sport's toughness—and, like any red-blooded female, had been known to admire the hotness of some hockey players like Ryan Guillemette and Zac Parotti—she couldn't really focus. What had she been thinking, virtually asking Jasper out, mentioning Joe's Diner?

That was a guarantee to have people point the finger, whisper about her more. It was hardly a private space. She groaned. She was such an idiot.

"What's wrong?" Jackson asked.

She could hardly answer that honestly. "I'm just a bit worried about facing people again."

"You mean tomorrow at church?"

She jumped on that excuse. "Yes." It remained true.

Mitchell glanced at her. "Hey, you don't need to worry. We'll be there."

"You're going to church?" Jackson asked. "Since when?"

"Since tomorrow." Mitchell's forehead wrinkled. "That doesn't make sense."

"None of this does," Cooper said, his socked feet on the coffee table, just missing the popcorn bowl. "What happened to Mitchell the Hockey God who's all about wine, women and song?"

"Are those computers frying your brain or what?" Mitchell scoffed. "I don't do wine, or song, and the women, well." He shrugged.

"Hey Coop, don't judge him for wanting to go to church," Ellie said.

Mitch reached out a hand to fist-bump her, his attention back on the game.

She met his fist with a light tap, hoping this would be the end of the conversation. But in the next break, Mitch glanced at her again. "I mean it. We'll be there. Nobody's gonna be asking you questions, otherwise they'll have to answer to me."

"Because you don't do scary ogre, right?" Cooper jeered.

Mitchell's grin flashed in his beard. "Only when it's necessary."

―――――

HER BROTHERS' support helped as they attended church with Mom the next day. Ellie sat with Cooper on one side, Mitch on the other, and she saw how his attendance—the first time since Christmas last year—instantly stole the spotlight from her. Sure enough, there were no questions asked about her, not when everyone wanted to ask one of Trinity Lakes' most famous exports about his thoughts on the NHL playoffs.

Whether he'd attended for Mom's sake, or for hers, or he'd

really found desire for relationship with God—something she'd prayed for but scarcely dared believe—she didn't know. But she was grateful, and relieved not to encounter any knowing smirks or tittered laughter.

She noticed Jasper there, with his mom and two older people who both bore some resemblance to his dad. But she didn't get a chance to speak to him, as he was surrounded by his own crowd of interested people, eager to learn about his father's health.

Mitch nudged her. "You gonna speak to him?"

In front of everyone here? "He's busy. I'll catch him later."

His mouth ticked up, then ticked a little higher as Georgia noticed them and lifted a hand. This of course drew Olivia's attention, and after acknowledging Mitchell's presence, with a dipped chin like a queen, she focused on Ellie.

"My granddaughter told me you felt unwell, Eloise. I'm glad to see you are feeling better."

"Thank you."

"I trust this won't hamper your efforts with the museum."

"No." She'd finish things by Memorial Day, even if it killed her. Although… She winced. "We'll do our best to make sure everything goes smoothly."

"I hope so."

She and Georgia offered small smiles and exited, and Ellie couldn't help but notice Mitch's gaze follow. Seriously?

Her eyebrows rose as she moved to face him, but before she could say anything he said, "What was that nose wrinkle about before when Mrs. Darcy asked about the museum?"

Oh. That. "Jasper was helping finish off some of the cabinets. And now with his dad's illness, and family staying in town, he's going to be so busy with the business that it's not fair to ask him to finish it off."

"I could help you."

"You?"

"I know my way around a power tool." He grinned. "And I

don't mean some of those knuckleheads on the ice."

Her smile poked out. "Since when?"

He shrugged. "Since forever. I've taken some classes, done some furniture restoration."

She blinked. Had the world gone crazy? "Are you for real?"

"Hey, a guy's gotta keep busy one way or another in the off-season."

"And here I was thinking you spent it traveling or playing golf."

"There's some of that too, but it gets a little lame sometimes."

And lonely, too, she guessed. Maybe that's why he'd not owned the skirt-chaser tag anymore. Maybe he wanted to settle down. Although why he couldn't just come home and be with the chaotic Reilly crew she didn't know. Or perhaps that was exactly why.

"Well, sure, if you're offering to help, that'd be awesome. But you probably need to check with Jasper."

"You better lead the way then."

She tensed. Talking to Jasper in front of everyone—including his extended family—felt fraught with potential misstep. Still, if it was the only way to ensure Mitchell's help, and not overburden Jasper…

She weaved through milling congregation members, smiling at Jodie Ladan, before reaching Jasper's family group. Jasper was talking to Brandon Taylor, so she waited, smiling at his aunt and uncle. They both glanced at her curiously, until Mrs. Cohen finished talking to Lynette Franklin and noticed her.

"Oh, Ellie." A hug. "And Mitchell too. Why, it's been a while since I've seen you."

He nodded. "Happy Mother's Day to you."

"Oh, thank you. It is because dear David is still with us, but it was a close call for sure."

"How is he?" Ellie asked.

"He can't wait to go home. But the doctors aren't sure and

want to do more testing, which may mean he stays for a few more days at least. Oh, Cindy, Frank," she turned to her relatives, "you remember Eloise and Mitchell Reilly, don't you? Jasper's friends."

Jasper turned at the sound of his name, smiling when he saw Ellie, a smile which faded a little as he nodded to Mitchell. "Hey."

Her brother held out a hand. "Jasper."

Ellie bit back a smile as they gripped hands. She wasn't sure if Mitchell had done it on purpose but that deep growl suggested a protectiveness designed to intimidate. He probably used it on the ice, too.

Mitchell's brow lowered. "I wanted to talk to you."

"Uh." Jasper's eyes shot to Ellie. "Sure?"

She nodded, and they moved to a quieter section. She hung back, not wanting it to be obvious she was talking to Jasper too.

Jasper glanced between them. "Can I ask what this is about?"

"You can."

"Oh for goodness' sake, Mitch. Give him a break." Ellie punched her brother's arm and turned to Jasper. "He wants to help with the museum exhibits."

"Thanks Ellie, I can talk for myself."

"Then talk."

She surreptitiously studied Jasper as he and Mitchell discussed the cabinetry. Jasper had seemed as surprised as she was to learn about Mitchell's skills—self-proclaimed, and Mitch had always been somewhat over-confident. Jasper shot her a glance, his blue eyes studying her, before he nodded at what Mitch was saying, and folded his arms.

Her heart thudded. Jasper might be a little shorter but he owned a handsome appeal in a completely different way to her brother. His gaze was thoughtful, his jaw only slightly square, and today it was dusted with dark stubble, as if he'd forgotten to shave last night. Her gaze trickled down to his biceps, and she figured he could give Mitch a good run for his money in an arm wrestle. Jackson, too. A glance over her shoulder saw Jackson talking with Lexi and her parents. He'd already made apologies for not being at lunch today as he was spending time with his in-laws to-be. Cooper was, as always, talking to Jess Martin who stood with her parents, the semi-retired veterinarian and his wife.

The room was filled with the buzz of conversations. Mom caught her attention, and Ellie nodded, shifting back to grasp Mitchell's arm. "We need to go."

He nodded. "I'll swing by tomorrow then."

"Thanks. I appreciate it." Jasper glanced at Ellie. "Catch you later?"

"Whenever you're free."

His nose wrinkled. "I can't see that happening any time soon. Unfortunately."

Disappointment surged. Then waned. She needed to be thinking of his best. Not hers. And his best was spending time with family, three of whom stood smiling at her, as if they were privy to information she didn't know.

Regardless, it made her long to escape. Preferably somewhere alone with Jasper so she could finally get the chance to talk with him and see if they could nudge the possibilities dancing around their friendship into something real. "Let me know when you're available."

"Oh, he's available," Mitch murmured.

Her cheeks heated to a color like that decorating Jasper's cheeks.

Mitch pointed at him. "Tomorrow."

"Sure."

"Don't do anything I would do."

"Mitchell!" She dragged her laughing brother away, mouthing a "sorry" over her shoulder at Jasper who was shaking his head.

Clearly, brothers had a lot to answer for.

————

THE DOCTOR EYED THEM SERIOUSLY. "I'm afraid that given the heart murmur, we're going to have to monitor you here for a few more days."

Jasper's heart sank and his mom exclaimed, "How long?"

"We need to rule out any complications." The doctor then went on a long tangent involving medical terms Jasper barely understood.

There were a lot of things he didn't understand these days. Like the medical world. Like Mitchell Reilly, of all people, actually possessing some carpentry skills. Like how Jasper could stand in a sea of people but only see one person. But she'd barely spoken to him on Sunday, nor he to her. He couldn't wait to finally see her alone, but when that would be was anyone's guess. Especially if his dad had to stay in hospital longer.

He clutched his jean-clad knees. But really, how could he even be thinking this way when his dad needed him at the hardware store? The past days seemed to have stretched longer as work piled up and he had to juggle care of the business with cares at home. Mom said she was fine, but he could tell she really wasn't. Uncle Frank might've returned to Dallas and Aunt Cindy was due to fly home tomorrow, but Mom was a little flighty, not quite focused. She needed him, whether she admitted it or not. Which meant delaying time with Ellie until his time was clear enough that he could think without distraction and focus just on her.

The doctor's discussion concluded, and he glanced at Jasper. "You look like you could do with some sleep, young man."

"I'm fine."

His next few days tracked ahead of him: work, hospital, driving Aunt Cindy to Pasco for her flight, then returning again.

"The doctor is right," Mom said later, on their trip back home. "You are looking weary. Are you sleeping okay?"

"Yeah." When he finally did. He'd spent far too long worrying for hours about Dad's medical expenses and how the arguments with the medical insurers would get resolved, and how much that would dent the hardware store's bottom line. When he did sleep it was to dream of a brunette with an infectious smile and laugh and to imagine what it would be like to kiss her. To have her kiss him.

"You've been working so hard." Mom patted his hand. "Such a good son."

"You know I love you and Dad."

"We do. But make sure you're not burning out. Take a night off soon, okay?" She smiled. "Maybe you and Ellie could finally go out."

He choked. "What do you mean by that?"

"I mean that your father is so bored lying in that hospital bed it seems he's decided to turn matchmaker. He might've just mentioned a certain message you'd received the other day."

"Man."

"Oh, don't blame him. I also saw the way you two looked at each other on Sunday at church, and Cindy might've mentioned something as well."

"What?"

She laughed, and he didn't mind being the cause of her mirth. It was the first time he'd heard his mother laugh since his dad's heart attack.

"I'll sort something out."

"Soon? You need to make the most of life, Jasper. This past week has taught us that more than anything."

He nodded. He knew that. And when he got home, he drew out his phone and sent Ellie another message. *Are you free Friday night?*

# CHAPTER SIXTEEN

Never had a week passed more slowly. Since receiving Jasper's text on Monday night, it seemed that time had slowed into a measure of seconds, each one dragging slower.

She'd cleaned up after the Mother's Day ranch stay guests. She'd organized more of the museum, and along with her brothers, been pleasantly surprised at Mitchell's skills.

Not to be outdone, Cooper had come on board too, offering skills and tech to make her video presentation of the Aussie sports a reality.

"This is so cool!" She pressed the red button that allowed thirty seconds of footage from an AFL game. This was followed by a cricket match which made no sense whatsoever. Peter Franklin had offered his voiceover, and she'd stayed up late way too many nights this week working with him to refine a script for him to record. Cooper had added this too, and the result was something with which she thought even Olivia would be well pleased.

But these were momentary distractions, as she could only focus on one thing.

Friday night. A date. Finally. With Jasper.

By the time Friday rolled around her nerves were threatening to burst from her blood vessels.

"Ellie, enjoy your time with Jasper," Mom said.

"But know you're gonna have to report back to us when you return," Cooper said.

"Can't wait," she said dryly. "Maybe I should've told him to take me to Vegas instead."

"Don't you dare," Mom warned, but with a twinkle in her eye.

"Why would she go to Vegas?" Mitchell asked.

"It's a long story," Mom said. "I'll tell you when she's gone."

Ellie had primped a little, done her best with her hair, and even worn one of the nice tops she'd bought while in Paris. The floaty pink lace number wasn't her usual speed, but it sure made a nice change from t-shirts and plaid and jeans.

She drove, wondering if she should've begged Jasper to pick her up, but then decided that she didn't want to put him through Mitchell's unsubtle interrogation. Mitch might be her second eldest brother, and think he was enlightened, but he still enjoyed the power to intimidate. And she wanted the evening with Jasper to go without a hitch. There'd been way too many hitches recently.

She parked, greeted the server and found the booth where Jasper already sat.

Talk about hitches. Her heart glitched, her breath suspended. He looked so handsome, in his pale blue button down and dark blue jeans.

He glanced up, his smile causing another seismic shift in her chest. Then he stood. "Hey stranger."

She hugged him, just like old times, but this hug felt like so much more. She couldn't linger like she wanted, conscious they were on show for half of Trinity Lakes. And while they'd done this—hugged, eaten here—a million times before, tonight felt like something special. Something new.

Marlene, the waitress who'd worked there since the dawn of time, drew close and handed them plastic-coated menus. "I could guess what it'd be, but then I could be wrong. It's been a long time since I've seen Miss Ellie here wearing make-up."

Did Marlene have to point it out? She'd hoped it was subtle, that it was enough to make her look prettier than she was, but not enough to draw attention to the fact.

"I think we'll need a few minutes," Jasper said.

"Take all the time you need, hon. I've got nowhere else I'd rather be." She winked and walked away, cracking her gum.

"Do you get the feeling we're tonight's evening show?" Ellie murmured.

"Want to go back to my place? We might get a moment's quiet considering Mom and Dad were hitting the hay early."

"Much as I'm glad your dad is finally out of hospital, I think they'd be glad for a night alone, don't you?"

"I actually don't want to think about that."

She laughed. "Okay, how about if I say I'd rather not run the risk of bumping into people we know."

"Then remind me why we're at Joe's Diner?"

"For the food?"

He exhaled. "So what, we eat and run, is that it?"

"We don't have to run," she said. "But maybe it won't hurt if it looks like everything between us is normal."

"But is it?" he asked. "What is normal anyway?"

He reached across the table to hold her hand. Her nerves soared and she pulled away.

"Okay, so holding your hand isn't normal," he said wryly. "But hugging is."

"Everyone is used to seeing me hug you."

"True." He studied her seriously. "But you know that I want them to also know it's normal for me to hold your hand."

Her pulse increased. So he still had feelings for her? After the past week she hadn't dared assume.

"I don't know why you still care about me," she murmured. "Not after all I did."

"Because what I feel for you is deeper than mere emotion. You know that."

"Jasper."

"So, have you two come to any decisions yet?" Marlene asked.

Her heart had. Even if the menu seemed a blur. "I'll get the usual."

"Trinity burger and a chocolate milkshake? Wait, that's your brother. You're a Trinity burger with onion rings, yes?"

"And a raspberry float."

"I want what she does," Jasper said, folding his menu and handing it to Marlene without taking his eyes from Ellie.

Her heart pounded.

"Yes, sir."

"Thanks Marlene."

He smiled, and Ellie's heart did a little fluttery dance around the outsides.

"Did I tell you that you look beautiful?"

"No."

"Well, Eloise Anne Reilly, you look beautiful."

"Thank you." She touched her hair. "I tried."

"You don't need to try. You're always lovely to me."

She ducked her head. How could he be so nice to her? How could she not have seen his many, many wonderful traits for so long? Now every one of his good qualities seemed to sing for her attention. His patience. His kindness. His loyalty. His work ethic. And yes, it didn't hurt that it was wrapped up in muscles that only reflected his inner strength.

"Jasper."

"Ellie."

His tease drew her smile. "Thank you for being so patient with me."

"Any time. That's what friends do, right?"

She wet her bottom lip, noticed his gaze flick to her mouth then back up again. Her heart pounded harder. Did he want to kiss her? She might have limited experience, but she knew now that was a sign of a guy's interest. "Is that all we are?"

He blinked. "Are you saying what I think you're saying?"

"That depends on what you think I'm saying."

He leaned closer, picked up her hand. "Are you saying you want to be more?"

"I... I don't want to wreck things between us again."

"You didn't wreck things," he assured. "That was me."

"You know I reacted that way because I was so surprised. And then Sebastian came almost immediately after, and I was confused, like I was tangled up in love and had no way of seeing reason."

"And now?"

"Now I see a lot more clearly."

"What do you see?"

"I see what kind of man I should hope for."

His nose wrinkled. "You should?"

"I do hope for."

The confusion in his face melded into a smile. "I think I like where this is heading."

"Because it's making you feel good? Careful, you'll start sounding like he-who-shan't-be-named."

"Non, non," he said in a terrible French accent. "Anything but zat."

She laughed, and shook her head. "I still feel like an idiot."

"You can't blame yourself. He fooled everyone."

"But not you. You knew something was wrong."

"I couldn't blame the man for liking you. I understood that only too well. But then when his story didn't add up, well, I couldn't let him hurt you."

His eyes remained on hers as Marlene placed their drinks on the table.

She didn't want to spoil this moment by looking elsewhere either. As soon as Marlene left, she whispered, "Thank you."

His gaze was soft. "You know I'd do anything to help you."

Her eyes filled. "I didn't see that at the time. I just thought I wanted to feel special and be loved."

———

HER WORDS CUT his heart deep. How could she think that? He squeezed her hand. "You know that I've always thought you were special."

Her hair fell in soft waves, obscuring her features as she ducked her head. Marlene returned, placed their food on the table, winked then moved away.

They ate, but her words kept eating at him, so when they'd finally finished their burgers, he returned to the matter so close to his heart.

"Ellie, what you said before, you know that you are loved."

She sighed. "I know I was desperate to be like the other girls I know and experience romance."

"Hey. That's nothing to be ashamed of. And you got a taste of it."

She slowly met his eyes again. "I'm so thankful it never went any further than kissing."

Breath he didn't know he was holding released. "He took advantage of you."

"That's what Georgia said. She said he was like Gary Wickley, d'you remember him? He preyed on vulnerable women too."

"For the record, I don't think you're too vulnerable."

"Just vulnerable enough?"

Gladness at her humor lifted his lips. "You're tougher than

you think. And hey, the past few months have proved you're human like the rest of us. We all make mistakes."

"Apart from you. When was the last mistake you made?"

He swallowed. Played with his plate. "I know there have been plenty since, but the one I can't forget is the one that changed everything with you."

"You mean...?"

"When I kissed you, yes."

She wet her bottom lip, and he suddenly wished they weren't in a diner in Trinity Lakes, but somewhere far more private.

"Did you really mean that?" she asked, toying with an onion ring.

"The kiss? Or calling it a mistake?"

"Either."

Wow, she certainly wasn't making things easy on him.

"I have both regretted and relived that kiss a million times since. I'm sorry that it hurt you, but not sorry to have finally known how soft your lips are."

"Jasper, I—"

He gripped her hand again. "Ellie, I love you. I don't want to wait a second longer for you to know that. And I'm serious. I'd do anything to protect you. Heck, I even faced your scary brother the other day and told him the same."

Her mouth fell open. "What did you say to him?"

"That he needed to back off hassling you about me and vice versa."

"Wow. You're so brave."

"That I am. But he had to know the truth. I'm yours, Ellie. I always have been, and I always will be."

Her face, forever beautiful to him, softened with something like adoration, and she placed a hand on her heart. Suddenly the lights in here seemed too bright, the background music too loud, and she was definitely too far away. He glanced at her plate. "Are you finished?"

"So finished," she said, without looking at it.

He smiled, as tension ratcheted up. "So am I."

He threaded her fingers with his, and like magic, Marlene appeared with their check. He paid it, adding a hefty tip, then they left with her good wishes for a great night.

"Where do you want to go?" He motioned to the lake, glimmering with silvery light.

"Too far," she murmured, hooking her arm inside his.

"The park?"

"Too public."

His lips curved. "Too public for what?"

Her smile flashed. "I can't tell you on the sidewalk with half of Trinity Lakes watching us."

"Got a better suggestion then?"

She nodded, grasped his hand, and tugged him in the direction of the museum. "Won't someone notice a light on?"

She shook her head. "I've been working all kinds of crazy hours trying to get this done."

"I can't believe it's been over a week since I've seen it."

"Well, you can see it now." She retrieved her key from her purse and smiled up at him. "Prepare to be amazed."

She unlocked the door then scurried in, switching off an alarm before gesturing him inside. Shadows stretched across exhibits, with only occasional splashes of light from the town street lamps spilling inside.

Even in the dimness he could see the progress in the past week, how the exhibits were now lined up, how the walls had been transformed with posters and signs.

"We had a minor issue with some fonts," she said, pointing to the Native American exhibit. "But Marianne soon got that sorted out." She tugged him to a far corner where new shelves held an array of hats and feather boas.

"What's this?"

"Our new dress up corner. Mindy's idea. It's supposed to increase the engagement with people, especially younger folk."

He found a hat—his mom might call it a bonnet—and placed it on her head. "Do you know who you remind me of?"

"Who?"

"That red-headed girl who lived in a place called something like Green Gables. Remember that movie Mom always liked to watch with you?"

"Do you mean Anne?"

"That's the one. Except you're not a redhead."

Her head tilted, toppling the bonnet to a precarious angle. "And how do I remind you of her?"

"Because you're so smart, and so fiery, and loving, and lovely." His hand traced her cheek.

"You know who you remind me of?" Her voice was husky. "Gilbert Blythe. Always faithful, always so good to Anne, even when her head was turned by another." Her hand reached to slide up his jaw. "She knew she didn't deserve him, yet he still proved himself faithful as Anne's Mr. Right."

He pressed a kiss in her palm. Through the shadows he caught how her pupils dilated. Heartbeat surging, he slipped his arm around her waist, as her other hand slid up his back. His head lowered until his forehead touched hers, and he closed his eyes. But he refused to move any closer, not willing to risk another mistake, needing her to direct things.

But then her breathy "Kiss me, Jasper," made her wishes plain, so he lowered the last inch, angling his mouth to meet hers in a kiss born of moonlight and dreams.

Ellie sank into his embrace, her chest pressed against his, as her hands slipped up to his neck and tugged him closer. She tasted sweet, like the sugary drink they'd recently had, the press of her lips igniting fire.

She sighed, like this was as perfect for her as it was for him, and the bonnet toppled to the floor. She twined her fingers in his hair as his hands slid up through hers, holding her as tenderly as a newborn. And this moment felt just as precious, something longed for, for *so* long. Priceless, treasured, cherished. "I love you," he breathed between kisses.

"I love you too," she murmured.

He inched back. "You do?"

"Of course." Her eyelids were heavy. "I always have." Her smile slid sideways. "And now I know I love you in a different way."

"What different way is that?" His tone was husky.

"This way." She closed the gap between their lips, and a new intensity flavored their kissing. Her hunger ignited his, and he crushed her closer, closer. She was still too far away, he wanted more, and she seemed only too willing to oblige.

Until the overhead lights flicked on and a throat was cleared behind them. "And just what's going on here?"

# CHAPTER SEVENTEEN

It was quite possible she was going to die of embarrassment.

She backed away from Jasper, picking up the bonnet and tossing it to the cushioned bench as she covered her swollen lips. Any lipstick that had survived dinner would've been kissed away by the best kisses of her life. Admittedly, her experience was limited, but Jasper's lips touching hers held fire and magic and promise. There was connection, sizzling connection yes, but something so much deeper, borne from a life of friendship strengthening into something new. Of course, trying to explain all of that to Sheriff Thompson right now was a little awkward.

"Don't rush to tell me. I'll make a best guess."

Beside her, Jasper chuckled, glanced at her then smoothed her hair. "Sorry. We were just—"

"Working on something," Ellie rushed to say.

"I could see that."

"And we got a little carried away," Jasper said.

"With the wonder of the museum, I bet."

Who knew the sheriff had such a dry sense of humor? "Sorry, sir. I didn't think we would be bothering anyone."

He snorted. "Try telling Rhonda Ingalls that. She saw movement here and thought she had to call the cops."

Bless her.

"But if it's just you two, and you're leaving soon," he eyed Jasper sternly, "then I'll go out there and tell her you were just doing some late night work, shall I?"

Jasper grasped Ellie's hand. "This wasn't work."

"So I gather." The sheriff's mouth twitched. He pointed a finger at Ellie. "Don't be too long. And maybe lock up behind me and go out the back. There's no telling how long Rhonda will stay out there despite the fact I'll do my best to get her to move on."

"Thank you." She offered a sheepish smile.

He smiled. "It's about time you made an honest woman out of her, young Cohen."

Her mouth sagged as Jasper insisted, "We haven't—"

Sheriff Thompson's wink stole the rest of his protest. Her shoulders relaxed.

"Now Ellie, while I've got you, we've got news on that French fraudster."

"Fraudster?"

He nodded. "The Feds picked him up in Arizona. Still with Kyla, who seemed determined to drag him to an altar, poor thing. She didn't believe it when she was told young Claud had tried this before."

"Claud? His name is Sebastian."

"Claud Sebastian Kuhl. He's wanted in France as well as several other places. He's tried that trick a few times before."

She sank into the cushioned bench seat. "What trick?"

"Wooing a pretty woman. Trying to get her money."

"But I don't have any money."

"With you the Feds are pretty sure he might've fallen in love, and wanted you to marry him and give him a green card. That's what he's said in his interviews, apparently. But I thought you'd like to know you don't need to worry about him anymore. And the fact there have been so many other women he's tried this with means you might not even need to go to court."

"And Mom's car?"

"From the charges he'll be facing I'm sure the insurance will pay out." He smiled. "It's early days, but I wouldn't be surprised to learn there was some kind of reward. There usually is when this kind of criminal is found, and seeing you're the one who brought him to our attention, it may well go to you." He pointed to Jasper. "Now, lock up and get her home. We don't want more tongues wagging around this place."

"Yes, sir."

"Have a good night, folks." Sheriff Thompson winked again and exited the front door.

She slowly exhaled, glanced at Jasper, who wore his own look of such immense relief that she instantly got the giggles.

"Stop it," he whispered, grinning.

"I can't help it. Oh my gosh, imagine if it had been Rhonda seeing us kissing like that."

"She'd need a fan and a fainting couch for sure."

"Fainting couch? How many old movies have you been watching, Jasper Cohen?"

"It's Mom and Aunt Cindy. Every time they get together they're always watching Jane Austen things and trying to explain it to me." He held up his hands. "There's only so much hockey I can watch before they drag me in with them."

"You poor thing."

He sidled closer. "You know it."

Her head tilted. "Do you want sympathy?"

"All the time."

He pressed another kiss to her lips, and she sank into his embrace when a rattle at the front door reminded her they hadn't locked it.

He broke away, and she rushed to the door and flicked the lock closed while Jasper reached to turn off the lights.

"Who's in there?"

She froze. That was definitely Rhonda's voice. They needed to leave. Pronto.

Ellie pointed to the alarm, then pointed at Jasper then the back door. He nodded and scampered to the back as she set the alarm. They now had thirty seconds to lock the back door and pull it closed before the alarm would blare.

They escaped out the back, and after making sure the door was secure, they kept hurrying through to the alleyway behind, which took them nearer the lake. It was cooler now, the night air hanging heavy with evening dew. They finally reached a park bench and collapsed onto it, breathing hard.

She burrowed into Jasper's side, reveling in his touch as he wrapped her in his hug. "That was insane."

"Almost busted by Rhonda Ingalls. Can you imagine?"

"I can't—I just—no."

He chuckled, drawing a hand down her hair. "Best date of my life though."

"Ditto."

"Best kiss of my life, too."

"Same."

As if the molecules in the air shifted between them there was a new charge in the air. He took his time kissing her, and she proved her love back through very thorough kissing of her own. Oh, how she loved this man. Loved his patience, loved his loyalty, loved his strength. "I love you, Mr. Cohen."

"And I love you, Miss Reilly."

And she sank against his shoulder and savored feeling cherished, safe, special, and deeply loved.

———

ALL THE NEXT week he struggled to keep the grin from exploding off his face. Ellie was his, and he was hers, and everything felt like it should be. Even Rhonda's questions put to Ellie at the museum the next day hadn't bothered them.

Rhonda had sailed into the museum while the volunteers were finalizing things for the grand opening on the weekend, then insisted on talking to Ellie. "I believe it was you who was here last night."

Ellie had nodded, and he'd done his best to not make it appear he was listening, as she said, "I did stop by, yes. I have been working some late hours this week."

"Rather too late, if you ask me." Rhonda sniffed.

"Nobody was asking you though, were they?" Mitchell had said, rising from where he'd been screwing in a fixture to secure a cabinet to the wall.

Ellie had bitten her lip, as if suppressing a smile. "Now, Ms. Ingalls, would you like a special tour or are you prepared to wait for the proper tour this weekend? Look at this fascinating exhibit about the first people in this area. See the artifacts we've collected? Don't you just love imagining what it must be like for someone to have held that in their hands hundreds of years ago?"

Rhonda's scowl suggested she didn't want a tour at any time, thank you, and she soon took herself off, but not without casting Jasper a squinty-eyed look that made him hope his face had appeared bland enough.

Mitchell's pointed look was harder to ignore. Jasper palms-upped him. Ellie's whisper in Mitch's ear saw him nod, smirk, then glance at Jasper again, this time pointing to the ring finger of his left hand.

Jasper's cough had drawn Mitchell's laughter, and Ellie's question of what was funny, was enough to send the hockey player into another fit of laughter. Jasper would have to have a word with Ellie. Her brother's cabinetry skills were okay, but not good enough to warrant that much teasing.

But even little things like that hadn't been enough to remove the smile from his soul. Dad was home and thriving, and the hardware store was going strong. It seemed many of the locals had decided to support his dad by supporting Cohen's Hardware, and while he was kept busy it was good to see the cash registers full.

And each day took them closer to the reopening of the museum.

---

JASPER STOOD NEXT TO MITCH, watching as Ellie took Olivia and Marianne around the exhibit. Behind them, a team of volunteer guides listened carefully as Ellie explained each exhibit with passion and clarity.

She drew near the Australian exhibit, inviting Olivia to press the red button for Ellie's pride and joy, the video.

"Oh, how marvelous!" Olivia's exclamation of surprise and delight drew Ellie's own look of beaming joy.

Jasper studied her, that smile that lit up his heart as well as it did a room. It wasn't just his grin that might explode. His heart might too, from pride in her.

"She really knows her stuff, huh?" Mitch muttered.

"She should study," Jasper murmured.

"Then why doesn't she?"

"Your mom's illness. The ranch. Money."

"Yeah, but those first two are dealt with now. And from what Sheriff Thompson said, she will be getting a reward, so what's stopping her?"

Jasper's heart stuttered. Oh. He hadn't realized what it would mean if she did study. He knew Ellie had done some online courses, but part of the appeal of university was the hands-on learning, especially for a history course, which may involve examining artifacts, and going places far from small town Trinity Lakes.

And while he was so glad to finally have Ellie near, that they were finally a couple, he loved her enough to want her to pursue her dreams. Even if that meant pursuing them far from home.

"What's wrong with you, dude?" Mitch asked.

Jasper shook his head. The movement seemed to alert Ellie's attention as she glanced in their direction. He nodded and smiled at her.

Olivia's attention shifted to him, and she offered her own nod, as if remembering what he'd done all those weeks ago. His stomach churned. What would happen if Ellie found out?

What would she do if she found out he'd paid for her wages for these past two months? Would she regard it as some kind of manipulation but on a whole other level to what Sebastian—Claud—had done? Nausea sloshed through him.

"Jasp, you look pale."

There was a good reason for that. And he bet his new bestie would be the first to fist-bump Jasper in the nose if he found out.

Which meant reminding Olivia not to tell anyone. Which meant somehow getting a look at the books and ensuring the treasurer had no paper trail that led back to him. Why hadn't he realized this until now?

"Dude?"

"I'm just gonna get some air."

He went outside in time to see Cooper talking with Jess Martin outside Joe's Diner. Cooper glanced across and lifted a hand, and he saluted back. He should leave. He should get back to work. Staying here was only inviting trouble.

"Jasper?"

He closed his eyes then turned, opening them to face Ellie.

"What's wrong? Mitch said you felt unwell."

"It's just something I forgot to do."

"If you need to leave that's okay. Everyone would understand, and we're doing okay here. And you've helped way beyond the call of duty." She smiled up at him.

Guilt streaked through his heart. How could he have gone behind her back like this?

"Eloise?" Olivia called.

He needed to speak to her. She was the key to all of this. If he could just convince her to stay quiet then all would be okay.

"You better go." He pressed a kiss to her cheek. How awesome that he could do so publicly now and no-one wondered any longer. "You're a popular lady."

"Are we still on for a date tonight?"

"Absolutely." Unless Olivia spilled the beans first. He hugged Ellie then released. "Sorry, I should scram."

"I better go too. Olivia has something she wants to talk to me about, and I'm a little nervous about just what that might be."

The trepidation riding his veins trebled. How he hoped it wasn't what he feared.

"Eloise?" Olivia Darcy called from the museum's entry. "Oh, and young Mr. Cohen. You're still here."

"Yes indeed."

She eyed him. "Can you stay a moment longer? I have something to say to Eloise, and I suspect it may concern you too."

"Oh, but—"

"It shan't take but a few minutes. Now, can you both come to the office, please?"

Ellie's eyebrows pushed up at him as she grasped his hand. Clearly neither woman would take no for an answer. Ah well. If Olivia admitted his involvement he would have to pray that Ellie could see the good intentions behind his decision and hope for the best.

And that she wouldn't stop looking at him like he'd hung the sun.

# CHAPTER EIGHTEEN

Ellie's chin rose as Olivia Darcy glanced at them both, then at their joined hands. Jasper moved to release hers but Ellie grasped it more firmly. Whatever Olivia had to say she could say to both of them. As a couple. A *couple*. She smiled.

"Right, well. I have to begin by congratulating you, Eloise. You have done what seemed impossible only a few months ago. And to see the results of your hard work, and those of talented people like your young man here."

Jasper straightened in his seat. His hand felt clammy.

Ellie glanced across at him. He wore a tight smile.

"I am most appreciative," Olivia continued. "And as I mentioned, I have a special opportunity for you."

Her heart tensed. What could it be?

"But before I get to that, I wanted to say thank you, Jasper, for your efforts and contributions in making this possible in the first place. Truly, without such vision it might not have happened at all. And certainly not with the speed and efficiency we have seen. You've done well, young man. I don't know what your motivation was, although one can guess." Olivia smiled a thin smile.

Jasper's vision? Mrs. Darcy was old. Surely she meant Ellie's vision. And what did she mean about his motivation? "I'm sorry, but I don't understand."

"Mrs. Darcy," Jasper hurried to say, "we had an agreement, and—"

"An agreement about what?" Ellie asked.

Silence filled the room.

"Forgive me if this is a stupid question, but is there something you're not telling me?"

Olivia's thin eyebrows shifted as she glanced at Jasper.

Ellie turned to him too. "Jasper? What's going on?"

He shook his head. "Nothing."

"Well, that's clearly not true." Her smile faded. "Is something wrong?"

"No."

"I see I have been precipitant," Olivia said. "Forgive me. Jasper, let me just say this: it is clear from the last financial projections that the museum will be solvent, and therefore the debt is paid."

"Mrs. Darcy—"

"No, please don't argue." She held up a hand. "It is fruitless. I discussed it with Marianne and we are of the same mind. You will find the exact amount in your account by close of business today."

His jaw dropped.

"What amount? What are you talking about?"

Olivia smiled. "Let's just say your young man here made a sizeable investment in the working capital of the museum, one that has clearly paid off." She eyed him sternly. "And it has been paid off. Understand?"

"Not really," he murmured. "But thank you." His lips quirked. "That money will go a long way to help pay for my dad's hospital bills."

Ellie studied him, releasing his hand. "Jasper?"

"Now, I really don't have time for any potential disputes, so as far as I'm concerned the matter is now closed. Eloise, earlier I mentioned an opportunity. Your enthusiasm for our local history demonstrates a passion for studies of this nature. I have been discussing with the board and with my grandson, Liam, who clearly has skills in the business arena, and we are all in agreement." She cleared her throat. "As you know the re-establishment of the museum was an initial role, funded by an anonymous donor."

Jasper inhaled sharply.

Ellie glanced at him. No…

"Well, given the success, we would like you to consider taking on the role in a more permanent manner."

Her breath hitched as suspicion about the identity of that donor was outshone by new glittering possibility. "You mean —?"

"I mean, we would like you to consider a role overseeing the museum in a permanent part-time capacity, which would of course permit time for you to continue your studies."

"My studies? I'm not studying, Mrs. Darcy."

"But you should be. That is evident to all. And a degree in historical studies is something that can help add a certain cachet to one's resume."

She winced. "I'm sure it would, but I don't have the financial means to support that."

"But you do."

"I beg your pardon?"

"You now do."

"If you mean the reward for Sebastian's arrest, I'm afraid that's supposed to take months to arrive, and even then, we may have to spend it on a new car for Mom."

"No, no. I'm afraid you don't understand."

Clearly not.

"Oh, I am a duffer. Did I not mention it? Your stipend forms part of a scholarship to the university of your choice." Olivia smiled. "Well, within reason of course. I'm afraid overseeing the museum from a place like Oxford or Cambridge might be rather a challenge. I know it's too late for next semester, for most places anyway, but I have some strings I can pull if you're interested in certain private establishments. Regardless, you could definitely consider studying in the spring semester, if you so wished."

Ellie covered her mouth with her hands. "Are you serious?" Was this an answer to prayers she'd felt had gotten lost in recent years?

"I've never been more serious in my life." Olivia glanced at Jasper. "I think there is at least one person sitting here who is hoping you might consider a more local college for your studies."

Jasper's lips tweaked up.

"I... I don't know what to say," Ellie stammered.

"I feel a sense of déjà vu." Olivia smiled.

Ellie laughed, but still couldn't believe it. "You're not pulling my leg? This isn't some leftover April fool's prank, is it?"

"My dear, I do not pull legs."

Jasper's smothered chuckle tugged out her own. "Georgia asked me to stay with her and study at Seattle University." She felt Jasper tense. "But I could study closer to home. That is, if you're sure."

"I have never been more so," Olivia said. "Of course, you do not need to accept the position if you would rather do something else. Only it would be rather a coup for our little museum if you were to say yes. One can always study part-time if one chooses. Or undertake a bridging course as you wait for the deadline for next semester. Really, the options are endless."

The possibilities really were endless. What could this mean for her—for them? "There is so much to think about."

"Of course." Olivia pushed a cream folder to her. "I have

taken the liberty of outlining some of the details in this document, and a contract you may wish to have your legal team look over."

Ellie's legal team? She nearly laughed again.

"Please let me know your thoughts at your earliest convenience." She glanced at Jasper. "And my thanks and congratulations to you again young man. You have certainly inspired much good, and I trust you will see your reward without much delay. Now, if you'll both excuse me? I have other business to take care of."

She smiled and sailed from the room like the grand dame she was.

Ellie turned as Jasper scrubbed a hand over his face. "Did she just say what I thought she did?"

"She said a lot." He exhaled.

"Did I hear her correctly when she said they wanted me to continue in a paid role, and I'd also be given a scholarship to study history at the university of my choice?"

"That's what I heard."

"Wow." She sank back in her chair, mind stumbling over this information. "I don't know what to say."

"Yeah, I would've thought that was obvious," he said. "You have to say yes, right?"

"Well yeah. But…"

He shook his head. "There is no but. You have to do this, Ellie. You know you want to."

"But if it means leaving you, I don't know—"

"No. I'm not going to be the reason you don't do college. You can study and we can still be together. We can make this work."

"But I don't want it to be work. It's taken so much to get here, I just want to enjoy being with you."

He gave a crooked smile. "And you can, and you can still say yes. When would next semester start?"

"The end of August."

"So we'd have three months before you'd have to go, if you got a place. And if you didn't, we'd have until next year. Either way, that'd be plenty of time to know whether this has legs to last."

"What do you mean? Of *course* it's going to last. You're my best friend. It's just that I don't want to do anything to jeopardize that again."

He shifted in his seat, turning his chair to face her directly. "And you won't. Unless you say no. Then there's a real chance you'll one day resent me for holding you back."

"That could never happen."

"Ellie, how long have you dreamed of studying history at school?"

She swallowed. How long had it been? Years? Nearly a decade?

"Do you remember praying, asking God to direct your paths? What if this is a God-given opportunity to do exactly that? I can't think too many people would say no to that."

But if leaving Trinity Lakes meant leaving him…

"Ellie." He took her hands again. "I love you and just want you to be happy. Please look this over and don't make any hasty decisions. We've got all the time in the world."

She drew in a shaky breath and nodded, which seemed to shake loose another thought. "Before, when she was talking about an anonymous donor."

He tensed.

"That was you, wasn't it?"

---

HE CLOSED HIS EYES. Then opened them and nodded.

Her eyes rounded. "What did you do?"

He shrugged, hoping she'd buy the casualness, but fairly

certain she wouldn't. "I contributed some funds, and may have suggested you'd make a good director of the history museum."

She blinked. "How much?"

He told her, and her mouth fell open. "Jasper."

"I didn't do it to try to make you stay, I promise. I just wanted you to find something that would tug at your dreams, and help you walk in your gifts and calling, and—"

She propelled from her seat and hugged him, fiercely, until it was getting hard to breathe.

"So that's not a bad thing?" he murmured against her hair.

"You wonderful, wonderful man." She clasped his face and studied him, before kissing him on his cheeks, his nose, his chin, jaw, lips. "I can't believe you would do that for me."

"I'd do anything for you." He kissed her then released her. "Even cheer you on as you studied in Seattle or Spokane."

Her eyes glimmered and she swiped at a tear. Then another. "Oh, I don't know why I'm crying."

"Hey, it's okay. Really. This is a good thing."

"I know it's a good thing. But I just can't believe it's happening to me."

The door opened and Mitchell looked in. "Ellie? Why are you crying? What's he done?"

"Nothing, man."

"He did everything," Ellie sobbed. "He paid for me to work here and would've kept it a secret except Mrs. Darcy just spilled the beans."

"You paid for her?" Mitchell eyed him.

"She needed the work and to get a taste for what's involved, so she could use her God-given talents."

Mitchell gave a thumbs-up. "Respect."

Huh. Well, okay.

Ellie's sobs continued. "And now he's saying he'll support me when I go study in Seattle."

"You're paying for that too? Wow. The hardware business must be booming."

"No, it's Mrs. Darcy. She's offered me a scholarship."

"That I had nothing to do with," Jasper clarified. "Ellie earned that all on her own."

"I don't deserve you."

He held her close. Glanced up at Mitchell with an apologetic grin then bent to study Ellie. "You deserve everything that is good in this world."

"And that's you." Ellie beamed up at him.

He kissed her hand. "That's you."

"That's me done. I'm out." Mitchell closed the door.

Finally.

Which left Jasper free to console his girlfriend in the best way he knew how.

With one of Ellie's own enormous bear hugs.

# CHAPTER NINETEEN

Gratitude filled Ellie as she looked around the milling throngs visiting Trinity Lakes' newly reopened historical museum. Around her, guides were discussing the various exhibits, leading visitors through the path from indigenous times to modern day. Hallie Hollaway and Jodie Ladan discussed the Bible college's history with Peter and Lyn Franklin. Ellie looked around, amazed at what they'd accomplished. It still felt like a miracle to be standing here with her mom and brothers, except for Dermott who, along with Mindy, had sent their best wishes from the Independence Islands.

"Pretty awesome, sis." Cooper wrapped an arm around her.

"He says that because he just wants recognition for his little video thingy," Mitch said.

"Little? I'll have you know that cost a pretty penny. You're just sore that people love that and barely give your furniture a second glance."

"Yeah, that's it entirely." Mitch rolled his eyes.

"Children, don't go spoiling Ellie's big day."

Ellie hugged her mom. Nothing was going to spoil this day. Everything was going perfectly. Cooper's sports video technology wasn't the only success. The Anzac biscuits were a knockout—already Marianne had needed to resupply the tray twice. The historical dress-up corner was also seeing plenty of takers, often to uproarious laughter as Georgia took photos that proclaimed #LoveTrinityLakes. Mitch had glanced that way a few times, she'd noticed.

He wasn't the only brother eyeing someone. Cooper was once again talking with Jessica, and Jackson couldn't keep away from Lexi. And as for her? She couldn't stop smiling whenever she thought about Jasper. Did ever such an impressive man exist?

"Have you thought anymore about what you'll do?" Mom asked.

She drew in a breath. Exhaled. Nodded.

"You'll make the right decision, I'm sure."

Again she nodded. God had good plans, and sometimes that meant stepping out into the unknown. But if He could orchestrate this, then He was sure to be faithful through it all.

Raised voices drew her attention out front to where Cooper stood with his hands on his hips as Jessica shook her head then pivoted and walked away. Whoa. Trouble in paradise? What was that about?

She glanced at Coop as he shook off Jackson's hand and stormed out the other direction. "Do you know what that was about?" Ellie asked her mother.

"I have no idea."

Jasper stole into view, holding a plate with several of Marianne's tasty creations. "Uh uh." He shifted it from Mitchell's grasp. "Wow, the people they let in here. Now there's one for you." He offered the plate to Mom. "And one to the queen of today's ball."

"Thank you." Ellie picked up a cookie—a biscuit, as the Aussies insisted it be called—and bit into the oaty-coconut goodness. "Yum."

"Right? I can see how eating these might make me a better soldier," Jasper said.

Ellie laughed.

"Yeah, because that's exactly what those poor dudes would've been thinking as they were getting shot at from all sides." Mitch bit into his own biscuit.

"It's good to see people are paying attention." Ellie smiled. "This is a place of learning, after all."

"Speaking of learning," Jasper said. "What are you thinking about your future studies?"

She swallowed the last biscuit mouthful and took his hand. "Can we go outside?"

"Sure."

She wove through the crowds, glad the earlier speeches were over and it was safe to steal away for a moment. They went out the back, out to where they could catch a glimpse of the lake gleaming under a late May sky. She gripped his hand and he tugged her near, close to his chest.

"Whatever you want, Ellie," he murmured into her hair. "I'm with you, one hundred percent."

"Thank you." She closed her eyes, wrapped her arms around his waist, and just breathed.

Slowly the world, the anxieties of the past weeks seeped away, as she closed her eyes and let his breath mingle with hers.

"Does this mean you've made a decision?"

She squeezed tighter. "You were right, you know."

"Mr. Right, that's me."

"That's for sure." She smiled.

"What was I right about?"

"Everything." She sighed. "I looked over the contract again, this time with Lexi and Cooper, and Mitch—they're all pretty familiar with things like that. It's such a good offer. Almost impossibly good, but Mitch's lawyer said it's legit."

"So?"

She felt him tense. She lifted her hand to his jaw. "So I'm going to take it."

He exhaled. "I'm glad."

She pulled back, studying his face. "You're sure you're okay about that?"

"Ellie, if I say I'm okay, then I am." His smile twisted. "Will it be hard being separated? Probably. But have we got a friendship that's weathered worse? Yes. And do we have a Heavenly Father who loves us, so that whatever happens we'll ultimately be fine? Absolutely."

She burrowed into his neck, pressing kisses against his skin. "I love you."

"And I love you." His head shifted, his chin angling until his lips found hers.

He kissed her and kissed her and kissed her until she laughed and pulled away and tucked her head under his chin.

He was right. About so many things. This world might be filled with flawed people, like Sebastian, and her runaway dad, herself, too, but God was still able to weave and work all things and bring good for the believer. God was a redeemer, able to fix the broken, heal the hurt, and bring the prodigal home. Whatever happened in the future, history had always shown that God was perfect, His love was sure, and that God would always direct their paths as they trusted Him.

She snuggled deeper. She would trust God, and trust Jasper. And trust that love would always win.


The End


Enjoyed this Trinity Lakes Romance?
Then check out the next in the series, *In Truth and Love* by Jenny Glazebrook
And stay tuned for Cooper's story in *Only You Can Love Me*.

# A NOTE FROM THE AUTHOR

Thank you for reading *Tangled Up in Love,* the ninth book in the Trinity Lakes romance series. Several years ago I was lucky enough to visit some gorgeous towns like Walla Walla and Chelan in Washington state, and it was fun to work with other authors to create a fictional town based on these places. If you've enjoyed this book, please check out the pictures from my visit to Washington on my website at www.carolynmiller-author.com

———

Reviews help other readers find new-to-them authors, so if you can spare a moment to write a quick review at Goodreads / your place of purchase, I'd be very grateful.

Make sure you check out Cooper's story in *Only You Can Love Me.* And if you've enjoyed this taste of small town life then read the Muskoka Romance series, that starts with *Muskoka Shores.*

If you enjoy Christian contemporary romance you may want to check out the books in the Original Six hockey romance series, a sweet & swoony, slightly sporty Christian contemporary romance series.

The Breakup Project
Love on Ice
Checked Impressions
Hearts and Goals
Big Apple Atonement
Muskoka Blue

Romance and hockey fans may also want to read *Fire and Ice*, the first book in the new Northwest Ice series, which may just have a book about Mitch, the final Reilly brother, and his quest to find love. (And you can find out about Dermott and Mindy's love story in the Independence Islands series, starting with *Restoring Fairhaven*)

I'd love for you to check out my other books and to sign up for my newsletter at www.carolynmillerauthor.com where you can be the first to learn all my book and contest news, and discover more behind-the-book details and photos. Newsletter subscribers can also get an exclusive bonus book free, so grab your copy of *Originally Yours* by visiting www.carolynmiller author.com today.

Next in the Trinity Lakes Romance series

Book #10 - *In Truth and Love* by Jenny Glazebrook

Jodie Ladan is tired of goodbyes. People have come and gone her whole life, and she refuses to be left behind again. It's time to take control, move to New York, and live out her dream of being a journalist. She's already been accepted into NYU and her plans are coming together.

Brandon Taylor's life is unravelling before his eyes. His mother is dying, he's seriously hurt a friend, and to add insult to injury, a distant relative is trying to have his father's house demolished.

Can anything else go wrong? Or can God use what others have meant for harm, for good?

Brandon and Jodie discover that when they speak the truth in love, God gives them every weapon they need to demolish the strongholds of the enemy.

Trinity Lakes is about to witness a battle for truth that only God can win.

Welcome to Trinity Lakes, the warm and welcoming small town in east Washington state filled with charm, family, and friends, where fresh starts, second chances, and romance abounds. You'll meet cowboys and swoony bachelors, sweet and sassy ladies, and your new best friends. This series of sweet and clean standalone Christian romances will warm your heart, inspire your faith, and bring a smile to your soul.

Check out the other books in the Trinity Lakes series:

Never Find Another You - Narelle Atkins

The Ocean Between Us - Meredith Resce

I'll Always Choose You - Lisa Renee

Always By My Side - Iola Goulton

Where Our Hearts Lie - Jenny Glazebrook

No Matter How Far - Sara Beth Williams

Over the Rainbow - Meredith Resce

Tangled Up in Love - Carolyn Miller

In Truth and Love - Jenny Glazebrook

Always in My Heart - Iola Goulton

Yesterday, Now and Always - Sara Beth Williams

Right in Front of You - Jessica Wakefield

Blue Skies Dreaming - Amanda Deed

# ABOUT THE AUTHOR

*Carolyn Miller lives in the beautiful Southern Highlands of New South Wales, Australia, with her husband and four children. A long-time lover of romance, especially that of Jane Austen, Georgette Heyer and LM Montgomery, Carolyn loves to write contemporary and historical romance that draws readers into fictional worlds that show the truth of God's grace in our lives.*

*To find out more about Carolyn's books, and to subscribe to her newsletter, please visit www.carolynmillerauthor.com. By subscribing, you can also get a free novella, Originally Yours.*

*You can also connect with her at*

# ALSO BY CAROLYN MILLER

<u>The Original Six hockey series</u>

The Breakup Project

Love on Ice

Checked Impressions

Hearts and Goals

Big Apple Atonement

Muskoka Blue

<u>Muskoka Romance series</u>

Muskoka Shores

Muskoka Christmas

Muskoka Hearts

Muskoka Spotlight

Muskoka Holiday Morsels

Muskoka Promise

<u>Northwest Ice hockey series</u>

Fire and Ice

The Love Penalty

Pointe, Shoots, and Scores

<u>Three Creeks Ranch Romance series</u>

A Cameo for a Cowgirl

<u>Trinity Lakes collection</u>

Love Somebody Like You

Tangled Up in Love

Only You Can Love Me

<u>The Independence Islands series</u>

Restoring Fairhaven

Regaining Mercy

Reclaiming Hope

Rebuilding Hearts

Refining Josie

Historical:

<u>Regency Wallflowers</u>

Dusk's Darkest Shores

Midnight's Budding Morrow

Dawn's Untrodden Green

<u>Regency Brides: Legacy of Grace</u>

The Elusive Miss Ellison

The Captivating Lady Charlotte

The Dishonorable Miss DeLancey

<u>Regency Brides: Promise of Hope</u>

Winning Miss Winthrop

Miss Serena's Secret

The Making of Mrs Hale

<u>Regency Brides: Daughters of Aynsley</u>

A Hero for Miss Hatherleigh

Underestimating Miss Cecilia

Misleading Miss Verity

'Heaven and Nature Sing' from the Joy to the World Christmas
novella collection

'More than Gold' from

the Across the Shores novella collection